**Nora Roberts** is the *New York Times* bestselling author of more than one hundred and ninety novels. A born storyteller, she creates a blend of warmth, humour and poignancy that speaks directly to her readers and has earned her almost every award for excellence in her field. The youngest of five children, Nora Roberts lives in western Maryland. She has two sons.

Visit her website at www.noraroberts.com.

*Also available by*

# Nora Roberts

**THE MACKADE BROTHERS**
The Return of Rafe MacKade
The Pride of Jared MacKade
The Heart of Devin MacKade
The Fall of Shane MacKade

**THE STANISLASKIS**
Taming Natasha
Falling for Rachel
Luring a Lady
Convincing Alex
Waiting for Nick
Considering Kate

**THE CALHOUN WOMEN**
The Calhouns:
Catherine, Amanda & Lilah
The Calhouns:
Suzanna & Megan

**CORDINA'S ROYAL FAMILY**
Cordina's Royal Family:
Gabriella & Alexander
Cordina's Royal Family:
Bennett & Camilla

**THE MacGREGORS**
The MacGregors:
Daniel & Ian
The MacGregors:
Alan & Grant
The MacGregors:
Serena & Caine
The MacGregor Brides:
Christmas Fairytales
The MacGregor Grooms
The Perfect Neighbour
Rebellion

**THE STARS OF MITHRA**
Stars
Treasures

**THE DONOVAN LEGACY**
Captivated
Entranced
Charmed
Enchanted

**NIGHT TALES**
Night Shift
Night Shadow
Nightshade
Night Smoke
Night Shield

**THE O'HURLEYS**
The Last Honest Woman
Dance to the Piper
Skin Deep
Without a Trace

Time and Again
Reflections and Dreams
Truly, Madly Manhattan
Table for Two
Going Home
Summer Pleasures
Engaging the Enemy
Dream Makers
Love By Design
Christmas Angels
The Gift
Winter Dreams
Risky Business
The Welcoming
The Right Path
Partners
The Art of Deception
The Winning Hand
Under Summer Skies
Irish Rebel
The Magic of Home
The Law is a Lady

# Nora Roberts

## Entranced

MILLS & BOON

Mills & Boon, an imprint of Harlequin (UK) Limited,
Eton House, 18-24 Paradise Road, Richmond, Surrey TW9 1SR

© Nora Roberts 1992

ISBN: 978 0 263 87185 2

029-0209

Printed and bound in Spain
by Blackprint CPI, Barcelona

For all my cousins, who, thanks to our parents'
belief in family, are too numerous to mention

## *Prologue*

He understood his power early. What coursed through his blood and made him what he was did not have to be explained to him. Nor did he have to be told that this gift was one not possessed by everyone.

He could see.

The visions were not always pleasant, but they were always fascinating. When they came—even when they came to a small child whose legs were still unsteady—he accepted them as easily as he accepted the sun's rising each morning.

Often his mother would crouch on the floor with

him, her face close to his, her eyes searching his eyes. Mixed with her great love was a hope that he would always accept the gift, and that he would never be hurt by it.

Though she knew better, on both counts.

*Who are you?* He could hear her thoughts as clearly as if she had spoken aloud. *Who will you be?*

They were questions he couldn't answer. Even then he understood that it was more difficult to see into yourself than to see into others.

As time passed, the gift did not prevent him from racing and running and teasing his young cousins. Though often, quite often, he strained against its limitations and tried for more, it did not keep him from enjoying an ice-cream cone on a summer afternoon, or from laughing at cartoons on a Saturday morning.

He was a normal, active, mischievous boy with a sharp, sometimes devious mind, a strikingly handsome face set off by hypnotic gray-blue eyes, and a full mouth that was quick to smile.

He went through all the stages that lead a boy toward manhood. The scraped knees and the broken bones, the rebellions large and small, the first jumpy heartbeat at the smile of a pretty girl. Like all children, he grew into an adult, moved away from his parents' domain and chose his own.

And the power grew, as he did.

He considered his life a well-adjusted and comfortable one.

And he accepted, as he always had, the simple fact that he was a witch.

## Chapter 1

She dreamed of a man who was dreaming of her. But he wasn't sleeping. She could see, with a perfect clarity that was extremely undreamlike, that he was standing by a wide, dark window, with his arms relaxed by his sides. But his face was very tense, very purposeful. And his eyes… They were so deep, so unrelenting. Gray, she thought as she twisted in sleep. But not quite gray. There were hints of blue, as well. The color of them reminded her of rocks hacked out of a high cliff one moment, and of the soft, calm waters of a lake the next.

Strange—how strange—she knew that his face was taut and tensed, but she couldn't see it. Just those eyes, those fascinating, disturbing eyes.

And she knew he was thinking of her. Not just thinking of her, but somehow seeing her. As if she had walked up to the other side of that glass, stood there looking back at him through the wide windowpane. Somehow she was certain that if she lifted a hand to that glass her fingers would pass right through it until they found his.

If she chose to.

Instead, she thrashed, tangling the sheets and muttering in her sleep. Even in dreams Mel Sutherland didn't care for the illogical. Life had rules, very basic rules. She firmly believed you were better off following them.

So she didn't reach for the glass, or for him. She rolled, almost violently, knocking a pillow to the floor and willing the dream away.

It faded, and, both relieved and disappointed, she dropped deeper into a dreamless sleep.

A few hours later, with the night vision tucked away in her subconscious, she snapped awake at the clattering bell of the Mickey Mouse alarm clock at her bedside. One expert slap silenced it. There was no danger that she would snuggle down in the bed and slide back into sleep. Mel's mind was as regulated as her body.

She sat up, indulging in one huge yawn as she dragged her fingers through her tousled cap of dark blond hair. Her eyes, a rich, mossy green she'd inherited from a father she couldn't remember, were blurry for only a moment. Then they focused on the twisted sheets.

Rough night, she thought, kicking her legs free of them. And why not? It could hardly have been expected that she'd sleep like a baby, not with what she had to do today. After blowing out one long breath, she plucked a pair of gym shorts from the floor and yanked them on under the T-shirt she'd slept in. Five minutes later, she was stepping out into the soft-aired morning for her daily three-mile jog.

As she went out, she kissed the tips of her fingers and tapped them against the front door. Because it was her place. Hers. And even after four years she didn't take it for granted.

It wasn't much, she thought as she limbered up with a few stretches. Just a little stucco building tucked between a Laundromat and a struggling accounting firm. But then, she didn't need much.

Mel ignored the whistle from the car that passed,

its driver grinning appreciatively at her long, leanly muscled legs. She didn't jog for her looks. She jogged because routine exercise disciplined the mind and the body. A private investigator who allowed either to become sluggish would find herself in trouble. Or unemployed. Mel didn't intend to be either.

She started out at an easy pace, enjoying the way her shoes slapped the sidewalk, delighted by the pearly glow in the eastern sky that signaled the start of a beautiful day. It was August, and she thought of how miserably hot it would be down in L.A. But here, in Monterey, there was perpetual spring. No matter what the calendar said, the air was as fresh as a rosebud.

It was too early for there to be much traffic. Here in the downtown area it would be a rare thing for her to pass another jogger. If she'd chosen any of the beaches, it would have been a different matter. But Mel preferred to run alone.

Her muscles began to warm. A thin layer of sweat gleamed healthily on her skin. She increased her pace slightly, falling into a familiar rhythm that had become as automatic as breathing.

For the first mile, she kept her mind empty, letting herself observe. A car with a faulty muffler rattled by, with no more than a token hesitation at a stop sign.

An '82 Plymouth sedan, dark blue. The mental list was just to keep in practice. Dented driver's door. California license Able Charlie Robert 2289.

Someone was lying facedown on the grass of the park. Even as Mel broke her stride, he sat up, stretched and switched on a portable radio.

College student hitchhiking cross-country, she decided, picking up her pace again even as she made a note of his backpack…blue, with an American flag on the flap…and his hair color…brown…and… *Name That Tune,* she thought as the music began to fade behind her.

Bruce Springsteen. "Cover Me."

Not too shabby, Mel thought with a grin as she rounded a corner.

She could smell bread from the bakery. A fine, yeasty good-morning scent. And roses. She drew them in—though she would have suffered torture before admitting she had a weakness for flowers. Trees moved gently in the early breeze, and if she concentrated, really concentrated, she could just scent the sea.

And it was good, so very good, to feel strong and aware and alone. It was good to know these streets and to know she belonged here. That she could stay here. That there would be no midnight rambles in a battered station wagon at her mother's whim.

*Time to go, Mary Ellen. Time to head out. I've just got a feeling we should head north for a while.*

And so they would go, she and the mother she adored, the mother who would always be more of a child than the daughter who huddled on the ripped and taped front seat beside her. The headlights would cut down the road, leading the way to a new place, a new school, new people.

But they would never settle, never have time to become a part of anything but the road. Soon her mother would get what she always called "Those itchy feet." And off they would go again.

Why had it always felt as if they were running *away,* not running *to?*

That, of course, was all over. Alice Sutherland had herself a cozy mobile home—which would take Mel another twenty-six months to pay off—and she was happy as a clam, bopping from state to state and adventure to adventure.

As for Mel, she was sticking. True, L.A. hadn't worked out, but she'd gotten a taste of what it was like to put down roots. And she'd had two very frustrating and very educational years on the LAPD. Two years that had taught her that law enforcement was just her cup of tea, even if writing parking tickets and filling out forms was not.

So she had moved north and opened Sutherland Investigations. She still filled out forms—often by the truckload—but they were *her* forms.

She'd reached the halfway point of her run and was circling back. As always, she felt that quick rush of satisfaction at the knowledge that her body responded so automatically. It hadn't always been so—not when she was a child, too tall, too gangly, with elbows and knees that just begged to be banged and scraped. It had taken time and discipline, but she was twenty-eight now, and she'd gotten her body under control. Yes, sir. It had never been a disappointment to Mel that she hadn't bloomed and rounded. Slim and sleek was more efficient. And the long, coltish legs that had once invited names like Stretch and Beanpole were now strong, athletic and—she could admit privately—worth a second look.

It was then that she heard the baby crying. It was a fussy, impatient sound that bounded through an open window of the apartment building beside her. Her mood, buoyed by the run, plummeted.

The baby. Rose's baby. Sweet, pudgy-cheeked David.

Mel continued to run. The habit was too ingrained to be broken. But her mind filled with images.

Rose, harmless, slightly dippy Rose, with her fuzzy red hair and her easy smile. Even with Mel's natural reserve, it had been impossible to refuse her friendship.

Rose worked as a waitress in the little Italian restaurant two blocks from Mel's office. It had been easy to fall into a casual conversation—particularly since Rose did most of the talking—over a plate of spaghetti or a cup of cappuccino.

Mel remembered admiring the way Rose hustled trays, even though her pregnant belly strained against her apron. And she remembered Rose telling her how happy she and her Stan were to be expecting their first child.

Mel had even been invited to the baby shower, and though she'd been certain she would feel awkward and out of place at such a gathering, she'd enjoyed listening to the oohs and aahs over the tiny clothes and the stuffed animals. She'd taken a liking to Stan, too, with his shy eyes and slow smiles.

When David had been born, eight months ago, she'd gone to the hospital to visit. As she'd stared at the babies sleeping, bawling or wriggling in their clear-sided cribs, she'd understood why people prayed and struggled and sacrificed to have children.

They were so perfect. So perfectly lovely.

When she'd left, she was happy for Rose and Stan. And lonelier than she'd ever been in her life.

It had become a habit for her to drop by their apartment from time to time with a little toy for David. As an excuse, of course, an excuse to play with him for an hour. She'd fallen more than a little in love with him, so she hadn't felt foolish exclaiming over his first tooth, or being astounded when he learned to crawl.

Then that frantic phone call two months before. Rose's voice, shrill and nearly incoherent.

"He's gone. He's gone. He's gone."

Mel had made the mile from her office to the Merrick home in record time. The police had already been there. Stan and Rose had been clutched together on the sofa like two lost souls in a choppy sea. Both of them crying.

David was gone. Snatched off his playpen mat as he napped in the shade on the little patch of grass just outside the rear door of their first-floor apartment.

Now two months had passed, and the playpen was still empty.

Everything Mel had learned, everything she'd been trained to do and her instincts had taught her, hadn't helped get David back.

Now Rose wanted to try something else, something so absurd that Mel would have laughed—if not for the hard glint of determination in Rose's usually soft eyes. Rose didn't care what Stan said, what the police said, what Mel said. She would try anything, anything, to get her child back.

Even if that meant going to a psychic.

As they swept down the coast to Big Sur in Mel's cranky, primer-coated MG, she took one last shot at talking sense to Rose.

"Rose…"

"There's no use trying to talk me out of this." Though Rose's voice was low, there was steel in it that had only surfaced over the last two months. "Stan's already tried."

"That's because we both care about you. Neither one of us wants to see you hurt by another dead end."

She was only twenty-three, but Rose felt as old as the sea that spread out beneath them. As old as the sea, and as hard as the rocks jutting out from cliffs beside them. "Hurt? Nothing can come close to hurting me now. I know you care, Mel, and I know it's asking a lot for you to go with me today…"

"It's not—"

"It is." Rose's eyes, always so bright and cheery before, were shadowed with a grief and a fear that never ended. "I know you think it's nonsense, and maybe it's even insulting, since you're doing all you can do to find David. But I have to try. I have to try just anything."

Mel kept her silence for a moment, because it shamed her to realize that she *was* insulted. She was trained, she was a professional, and here they were cruising down the coast to see some witch doctor.

But she wasn't the one who had lost a child. She wasn't the one who had to face that empty crib day after day.

"We're going to find David, Rose." Mel took her hand off the rattling gearshift long enough to squeeze Rose's chilled fingers. "I swear it."

Instead of answering, Rose merely nodded and turned her head to stare out over the dizzying cliffs. If they didn't find her baby, and find him soon, it would be all too easy just to step out over one of those cliffs and let go of the world.

He knew they were coming. It had nothing to do with power. He'd taken the phone call from the shaky-voiced, pleading woman himself. And he was still cursing himself for it. Wasn't that why he had an unlisted number? Wasn't that why he had one of those handy machines to answer his calls whenever anyone dug deep enough to unearth that unlisted number?

But he'd answered that call. Because he'd felt he had to. Known he had to. So he knew they were coming, and he'd braced himself to refuse whatever they would ask of him.

Damn it, he was tired. He'd barely gotten back to his home, to his life, after three grueling weeks in Chicago helping the police track down what the press had so cleverly dubbed the South Side Slicer.

And he'd seen things, things he hoped he'd never see again.

Sebastian moved to the window, the wide window that looked out over a rolling expanse of lawn, a colorful rockery, and then a dizzying spill of cliffs dropping down to the deep sea.

He liked the drama of the view, that dangerous drop, the churning water, even the ribbon of road that sliced through the stone to prove man's wiliness, his determination to move on.

Most of all, he liked the distance, the distance that provided him relief from those who would intrude, not only on his space, but also on his thoughts.

But someone had bridged that distance, had already intruded, and he was still wondering what it meant.

He'd had a dream the night before, a dream that

he'd been standing here, just here. But there had been a woman on the other side of the glass—a woman he wanted very badly.

But he'd been so tired, so used up, that he hadn't gathered up the force to focus his concentration. And she'd faded away.

Which, at the moment, was just fine with him.

All he really wanted was sleep, a few lazy days to tend his horses, toy with his business, interfere in the lives of his cousins.

He missed his family. It had been too long this time since he'd been to Ireland to see his parents, his aunts and uncles. His cousins were closer, only a few miles down that winding cliff road, but it felt like years rather than weeks, since he'd seen them.

Morgana was getting so round with the child she carried. No, children. He grinned to himself, wondering if she knew there were twins.

Anastasia would know. His gentler cousin knew all there was to know about healing and folk medicines. But Ana would say nothing unless Morgana asked her directly.

He wanted to see them. Now. He even had a hankering to spend some time with his brother-in-law, though he knew Nash was hip-deep in his new screenplay. Sebastian wanted to hop on his bike, rev it up and whoosh up to Monterey and surround himself with family and the familiar. He wanted, at all costs, to avoid the two women who were even now heading up the hill toward him. Coming to him with needs and pleas and hopelessness.

But he wouldn't.

He wasn't an unselfish man, and he never claimed he was. He did, however, understand the responsibilities that went hand in hand with his gift.

You couldn't say yes to everyone. If you did, you'd go quietly mad. There were times when you said yes, then found your way blocked. That was destiny. There were times when you wanted to say no, wanted desperately to say no, for reasons you might not understand. And there were times when what you wanted meant nothing compared to what you were meant to do.

That, too, was destiny.

He was afraid, uncomfortably afraid, that this was one of those times when his desires meant nothing.

He heard the car straining its way up his hill before he saw it. And nearly smiled. Sebastian had built high and built solitary, and the narrow, rutted lane leading up to his home was not welcoming. Even a seer was entitled to some privacy. He spotted the car, a smudge of dull gray, and sighed.

They were here. The quicker he turned them back, the better.

He started out of the bedroom and down the steps, a tall man, nearly six-five in his booted feet, lean of hip and wide of shoulder. His black hair swept dramatically back from his forehead and fell over the collar of his denim shirt, curling a bit there. His face was set in what he hoped were polite but inaccessible lines. The strong, prominent bones gifted to him by his Celtic ancestors jutted against skin made dusky by his love of the sun.

As he walked down, he trailed a hand along the silky wood of the banister. He had a love for texture, as well, the smooth and the rough. The amethyst he wore on one hand winked richly.

By the time the car had chugged its way to the top of the drive and Mel had gotten over her first astonishment at the sight of the eccentric and somehow fluid structure of wood and glass he called home, Sebastian was standing on the porch.

It was as if a child had tossed down a handful of blocks and they had landed, by chance, in a fascinating pattern of ledges that had then fused together. That was what she thought as she stepped out of the car and was assaulted by the scents of flowers, horses and the trailing wind from the sea.

Sebastian's gaze flicked over Mel, and lingered a moment as his eyes narrowed. With the faintest of frowns, he looked away and focused on Rose.

"Mrs. Merrick?"

"Yes. Mr. Donovan." Rose felt a bubble rise to her throat that threatened to boil into a sob. "It's so kind of you to see me."

"I don't know if it's kind or not." He hooked his thumbs in the front pockets of his jeans as he studied them. Rose Merrick wore a plain, painfully neat blue dress that hung a bit on her hips. As if she'd recently lost weight. She'd taken some care with her makeup, but, judging by the way her eyes were shining, it wouldn't last long.

He struggled against sympathy.

The other woman hadn't bothered overmuch with appearances, which made her all the more intriguing. Like Sebastian, she was wearing jeans and boots, both well used. The T-shirt she'd tucked into the waistband of her jeans had probably been a bright red at one time, but was now faded with many washings. She wore no jewelry, no cosmetics. What she did wear—and Sebastian saw it as clearly as he did the color of her hair and eyes— was attitude. *Bad* attitude.

*You're a tough one, aren't you...* He scanned for

her name and was thudded by a whirl of feeling—a kind of mental static—that told him this one was in as much emotional turmoil as Rose Merrick.

Terrific.

Rose was already moving forward. Sebastian was trying to stand aside, to remain dispassionate, but he knew he was losing. She was fighting those tears, the ones he could feel burning out of her heart.

There was nothing on earth that weakened a man like a courageous woman.

"Mr. Donovan. I won't take up much of your time. I just need…"

Even as her words trailed off, Mel was by her side. The look she shot at Sebastian was anything but friendly. "Are you going to let us come in and sit down, or are we just going to…"

Now she was the one whose words trailed off. It wasn't threatening tears that robbed her of her voice. It was utter shock.

His eyes. It was all she could think for an instant, and indeed she thought it so clearly, so violently, that Sebastian heard the words echo in his own mind.

Ridiculous, she told herself, regaining control, It was a dream. That was all. Some silly dream she was mixing up with reality. It was just that he had the most beautiful eyes. The most uncomfortably beautiful eyes.

He studied her for a moment more, and, though curious, he didn't look beyond her face. She was, even in the harsh sunlight, quite attractive. Perhaps it was the defiance he saw so clearly in her steady green eyes, or the lift of her chin, with its faint and oddly sexy cleft. Attractive, yes, he decided, even if she did wear her hair inches shorter than his own. Even if it did look as though she hacked at it herself with a pair of kitchen shears.

He turned away from her and offered Rose a smile.

"Please, come in," he said, and gave her his hand. He left Mel to follow.

She did, and he might have been amused to see the way she swaggered up those steps and into the high-ceilinged great room, with its skylights and open balcony. She frowned a bit, wishing she didn't find it so appealing, those warm, honey-toned walls that made the light so soft and sexy. There was a low, wide couch, long as a river, done in a lustrous royal blue. He led Rose to it, over a lake-sized rug of bleeding pastels, while Mel checked out his living quarters.

It was neat as a pin without appearing viciously organized. Modern sculptures of marble, wood and bronze were interspersed with what were surely valuable antiques. Everything was large scale, with the result that, despite its size, the room was cozy.

Here and there, set with apparent casualness on those polished antiques, were clusters of crystals— some large enough to strain a man's back lifting them, others tiny enough to fit in a child's palm. Mel found herself charmed by them, the way they winked and gleamed, shaped like ancient cities, slender wands, smooth globes or rough mountains.

She found Sebastian watching her with a kind of patient amusement, and she shrugged. "Some digs."

His lips curved, joining the humor in his eyes. "Thanks. Have a seat."

The couch might be as long as a river, but she chose a chair across the island of an ornately carved coffee table.

His eyes stayed on Mel another moment, and then he turned to Rose. "Can I get you some coffee, Mrs. Merrick? Something cold?"

"No. No, please don't bother." The kindness was worse, somehow, undermining her desperate control. "I know this is an imposition, Mr. Donovan. I've read about you. And my neighbor, Mrs. Ott, she said how you were so helpful to the police last year when that boy went missing. The runaway."

"Joe Cougar." Sebastian sat beside her. "Yes, he

thought he'd give San Francisco a try, and drive his parents crazy. I suppose youth enjoys risks."

"But he was fifteen." Rose's voice broke and pressing her lips together, she shored it up again. "I—I don't mean his parents wouldn't have been frightened, but he was fifteen. My David's only a baby. He was in his playpen." She sent Sebastian a look of desperate pleading. "I only left him for a minute when the phone rang. And he was right by the door, sleeping. It wasn't as if he was out on the street, or left in a car. He was right by the open door, and I was only gone a minute."

"Rose." Though her personal preference was to keep her distance from Sebastian, Mel got up to sit beside her friend. "It's not your fault. Everyone understands that."

"I left him," Rose said flatly. "I left my baby, and now he's gone."

"Mrs. Merrick. Rose. Were you a bad mother?" Sebastian asked the question casually, and saw the horror bloom in Rose's eyes. And the fury light in Mel's.

"No. No. I love David. I only wanted to do my best for him. I only—"

"Then don't do this." He took her hand, and his touch was so gentle, so comforting, that the threatening tears retreated a little. "You're not to blame for this. Trying to make it so you are won't help find David."

Mel's fury fizzled out like a wet firecracker. He'd said exactly the right thing, in exactly the right way.

"Will you help me?" Rose murmured. "The police are trying. And Mel...Mel's doing everything she can, but David's still gone."

Mel, he mused. An interesting name for a long, slim blonde with a chip on her shoulder.

"We're going to get David back." Agitated, Mel sprang up again. "We have leads. They may be slim, but—"

"We?" Sebastian interrupted. He got a quick image—here, then gone—of her with a gun gripped in both hands, her eyes as cold as frozen emeralds. "Are you with the police, Miss—?"

"Sutherland. Private." She snapped the words at him. "Aren't you supposed to know things like that?"

"Mel..." Rose said with quiet warning.

"That's all right." He patted Rose's hand. "I can look, or I can ask. With relative strangers, it's more polite to ask than to intrude, don't you think?"

"Right." With what was certainly a snort, Mel dropped into a chair again.

"Your friend's a cynic," Sebastian commented. "Cynicism can be very valuable, as well as very rude." He started to steel himself to tell Rose he couldn't help. He simply couldn't open himself to the trauma and risk of looking for another lost little boy.

Mel changed everything. Just, he supposed, as she was meant to.

"I don't consider it cynicism to recognize a charlatan masquerading as a samaritan." Her eyes were hot when she leaned forward. "This psychic business is as phony as a ten-dollar magician in a shiny suit pulling rabbits out of his hat."

His brow quirked. It was the only sign of interest or irritation. "Is that so?"

"A scam's a scam, Mr. Donovan. A young child's future is at stake, and I won't have you playing your mumbo-jumbo games to get your name in the papers. I'm sorry, Rose." She stood, almost vibrating with anger. "I care about you, and I care about David. I just can't stand by and watch this guy hose you."

"He's my baby." The tears Rose had been battling spilled over. "I have to know where he is. I have to know if he's all right. If he's scared or happy. He doesn't even have his teddy bear." Rose buried her face in her hands. "He doesn't even have his teddy bear."

Mel cursed herself, cursed her temper, cursed Sebastian Donovan, cursed the world in general. But when she knelt beside Rose, both her hands and voice were gentle.

"I'm sorry. Honey, I'm sorry. I know how scared you are. I'm scared, too. If you want Mr. Donovan to—" she almost choked on the word "—to help, then he'll help." She raised her furious, defiant face to Sebastian's. "Won't you?"

"Yes." He nodded slowly, feeling fate take his hands. "I will."

He managed to persuade Rose to drink some water and dry her eyes. While Mel stared grimly out the window, Rose took a small yellow teddy bear out of her bag.

"This is David's. His favorite. And this…" She fumbled with a wallet sized snapshot. "This is his picture. I thought— Mrs. Ott said you might need something."

"It helps." He took the toy and felt a vicious pull in his gut that he recognized as Rose's grief. He would have to go through, and beyond, that. But he didn't look at the photograph. Not yet. "Leave it with me. I'll be in touch." He helped her to her feet. "You have my word. I'll do what I can."

"I don't know how to thank you. For trying. Just knowing you are… Well, it gives me something else to hope for. We, Stan and me, we've got some money saved."

"We'll talk about it later."

"Rose, wait in the car for me," Mel said it quietly, but Sebastian could see that she was feeling anything but quiet. "I'll pass on what information I have to Mr. Donovan. It may help him."

"All right." A smile ghosted around Rose's mouth. "Thank you."

Mel waited until Rose was out of earshot, then turned and fired. "How much do you think you can squeeze out of her for this kind of a con? She's a waitress. Her husband's a mechanic."

He leaned lazily against the doorjamb. "Ms. Sutherland, does it appear I need money?"

She made another derisive sound. "No, you've got just buckets, don't you? It's all just a game for you."

He curled his fingers around her arm with a steely strength that caught her off guard. "It's not a game." His voice was so low, so filled with suppressed violence, that she blinked. "What I have, what I am, is no game. And stealing children from their playpens is no game, either."

"I won't see her hurt again."

"We can agree on that. If you're so against this, why did you bring her?"

"Because she's my friend. Because she asked me to."

He accepted that with a slight nod. Loyalty was something else he could feel pumping out of her. "And my private number? You dug that up, as well?"

Her lip curled in something close to a sneer. "That's my job."

"And are you good at it?"

"Damn right."

"Fine. I'm also good at mine, and we're going to be working together."

"What makes you think—?"

"Because you care. And if there's a chance—oh, even the slimmest chance—that I'm what I claim to be, you won't want to risk ignoring it."

She could feel the heat from his fingers. It seemed to sizzle right through the skin to her bones. It occurred to her that she was afraid. Not physically. It was deeper than that. She was afraid because she'd never felt this kind of power before.

"I work alone."

"So do I," he said calmly. "As a rule. We're going to break the rules." He reached in, quick as a snake. He wanted one thing, one small thing, to rub her nose in. Finding it, he smiled. "I'll be in touch very soon. Mary Ellen."

He had the pleasure of seeing her mouth fall open,

of seeing her eyes narrow as she thought back, struggling to remember if Rose had used her full name. But she couldn't remember, couldn't be sure. Shaken, she jerked away.

"Don't waste my time, Donovan. And don't call me that." With a toss of her head, she strode to the car. She might not be psychic, but she knew he was grinning.

## Chapter 2

Sebastian didn't go back inside, not even after he had watched the little gray car trail down the ribbon of Highway 1. He stood on the porch, both amused and faintly irritated by the sizzles of anger and frustration Mel had left behind to spark in the air.

Strong-willed, he mused. And just brimming with energy. A woman like that would exhaust a peaceful man. Sebastian considered himself a peaceful man. Not that he wouldn't mind poking at her a bit, the way a young boy pokes at glowing embers to see how often he can get a flame to shoot up.

It was often worth the risk of a few minor burns to make fire.

At the moment, however, he was just too tired to enjoy it. He was already angry with himself for having agreed to become involved. It was the combination of the two women that had done it to him, he thought now. The one with her face so full of fears and desperate hope, the other so vivid with fury and sneering disbelief. He could have handled one or the other, he thought as he descended the steps. But being caught in the middle of all that conflicting emotion, the sheer depth of it, had defeated him.

So he would look. Though he had promised himself a long, quiet break before taking on another case, he would look. And he would pray to whatever god was listening that he could live with what he might see.

But for now, he would take some time—one long, lazy morning—to heal his fatigued mind and ragged soul.

There was a paddock behind the house, attached to a low, gleaming white stable. Even as he approached, he heard the whicker of greeting. The sound was so ordinary, so simple and welcoming that he smiled.

There they were, the sleek black stallion and the proud white mare, standing so still that he thought of two elegantly carved chess pieces, one ebony, one alabaster. Then the mare flicked her tail in a flirtatious gesture and pranced to the fence.

They could leap it, he knew. Both had done so more than once, with him in the saddle. But there was a trust between them, an understanding that the fence was not a cage but a home.

"There's a beauty." Sebastian lifted a hand to stroke her cheek, her long, graceful neck. "Have you been keeping your man in line, Psyche?"

She blew into his hand. In her dark eyes he saw pleasure, and what he liked to think was humor. She whinnied softly when he swung over the fence. Then she stood patiently while he passed his hands over her flanks, down over her swollen belly.

"Only a few more weeks," he murmured. He could almost feel the life inside her, sleeping. Again he thought of Morgana, though he doubted his cousin would care to be compared to a pregnant horse, even as fine an Arabian as Psyche.

"Has Ana been taking good care of you?" He nuzzled against the mare's neck, comforted by her quiet good nature. "Of course she has."

He murmured and stroked for a while, giving her the attention they had both missed while he'd been away. Then he turned and looked at the stallion, who stood alert, his handsome head high.

"And you, Eros, have you been tending to your lady?"

At the sound of his name, the horse reared to paw the air, trumpeting a cry that was rich in power and almost human. The display of pride had Sebastian laughing as he crossed to the stallion.

"You've missed me, you gorgeous beast, admit it or not." Still laughing, Sebastian slapped the gleaming flank and sent Eros dancing around the paddock. On the second trip around, Sebastian grabbed a handful of mane and swung onto the restless mount, giving them what they both wanted. A fast, reckless ride.

As they soared over the fence, Psyche watched them, her eyes as indulgent—and as superior—as a mother watching little boys wrestling.

Sebastian felt better by the afternoon. The hollowness he'd brought back from Chicago was gradually being filled. But he continued to avoid the little yellow teddy bear sitting lonely on the long, empty sofa. And he had yet to look at the photograph.

In the library, with its coffered ceiling and its walls of books, he sat at a massive mahogany desk and toyed with some paperwork. At any given time, Sebastian might have between five and ten businesses of which he was either sole owner or majority partner. They were hobbies to him—real estate, import-export firms, magazines, a catfish farm in Mississippi that amused him, and his current pet, a minor-league baseball team in Nebraska.

He was shrewd enough to make a healthy profit, wise enough to leave day-to-day management in the hands of experts, and capricious enough to buy and sell on a whim.

He enjoyed what money could give him, and he often used those profits lavishly. But he had grown up with wealth, and amounts of money that would have startled many were hardly more than numbers on paper to him. The simple game of mathematics, the increasing or decreasing, was a never-ending source of entertainment.

He was generous with pet charities, because he believed in them. His donations were a matter not of tax breaks or philanthropy, but of morals.

It would probably have embarrassed him, and it would certainly have irritated him, to be thought of as an unshakably moral man.

He pleased himself until sunset, working, reading, toying with a new spell he hoped to perfect. Magic was his cousin Morgana's speciality. Sebastian could never hope to equal her power there, but his innate competitive streak kept him struggling to try.

Oh, he could make fire—but that was a witch's first and last skill. He could levitate, but that, too, was an elementary talent. Beyond that and a few hat tricks—that was Mel sneaking back into his mind again—he was no magician. His gift was one of sight.

In much the same way that a brilliant actor might yearn to sing and dance, Sebastian yearned to cast spells.

After two hours with little success, he gave up in disgust. He fixed himself an elaborate meal for one, put some Irish ballads on the stereo and uncorked a three-hundred-dollar bottle of wine with the same casualness another man might show in popping open a can of beer.

He indulged in a lengthy whirlpool, his eyes closed, his mind a blessed blank as the water jetted around him. After slipping into silk pajama bottoms, he pleased himself by watching the sun set in bleeding reds. And then he waited for night to steal across the sky.

It couldn't be put off any longer. With some reluctance, Sebastian went downstairs again. Rather than flick on lights, he lit candles. He didn't need the trappings of the art, but there was comfort in tradition.

There was the scent of sandalwood and vanilla. Because they reminded him of his mother's room at Castle Donovan, they never failed to soothe him. The light was shadowy, inviting power.

For several long moments, he stood by the sofa. With a sigh—very like a laborer might make on hefting a pick—he looked at the photograph of David Merrick.

It was a charming, happy face, one that would have made Sebastian smile if his concentration hadn't been focused. Words gathered in his head, ancient words, secret words. When he was sure, he set the picture aside and lifted the sad-eyed yellow bear.

"All right, David," he murmured, and his voice echoed hollowly through the empty rooms. "Let me see."

It didn't happen with a blaze of light or a flash of understanding. Though it could. It could. He simply drifted. His eyes changed, from smoke to slate to the color of storm clouds. They were fixed, unblinking, beyond the room, beyond the walls, beyond the night.

Images. Images. Forming and melting like wax through his mind. His fingers were gentle on the child's toy, but his body had stiffened like stone. His breathing remained steady, slowing, evening out as it would in sleep.

To begin, he had to fight past the grief and fear that shimmered through the toy. Without losing concentration, he had to slip past the visions of the weeping mother clutching the bear, of a dazed-eyed father holding them both.

Oh, but these were strong, these emotions of sorrow and terror and fury. But strongest of all, as always, was the love.

Even that faded as he skimmed past, going deeper, going back.

He saw, with a child's eyes, and a child's wonder.

A pretty face, Rose's face, leaning over the crib. A smile, soft words, soft hands. Great love. Then another, a man's face, young, simple. Hesitant fingers, rough and callused. Here, too, was love. Slightly different from the mother love, but just as deep. This was tinted with a kind of dazed awe. And... Sebastian's lips curved. And a wish to play catch in a nice backyard.

The images slid, one into the other. Fussy crying at night. Formless fears, soon soothed by strong, caring hands. Nagging hungers sated by warm mother's milk from a willing breast. And pleasures, such delight in colors, in sounds, in the warmth of sunlight.

Health, robust health, in a body straining to grow as a babe's did in that first dazzling year of life.

Then heat, and a surprising, baffling pain. Aching, throbbing in the gums. The comfort of being walked, rocked, sung to.

And another face, soft with a different kind of love. Mary Ellen, making the yellow bear dance in front of his eyes. Laughing, her hands tender and hesitant as she gathered him up, holding him high in the air and pressing tickling kisses to his belly.

From her, a longing, too unformed in her own mind to be seen clearly. All emotion and confusion.

What is it you want? Sebastian wanted to ask her. What is it you're afraid you can't have?

Then she faded away from him like a chalk portrait washed away in a shower of rain.

Sleeping. Dreaming easy dreams, with a slash of sunlight just beyond your fisted hand and the shade cool and soft as a kiss. Peace, utter peace.

When it was broken, there was sleepy irritation. Small, healthy lungs filled to cry, but the sound was cut off by a hand. Unfamiliar hands, unfamiliar smell, and then irritation turned to fear. The face— There was only a glimpse, and Sebastian struggled to freeze that image in his mind for later.

Being carried, held too tightly, and bundled in a car. The car smells of old food and spilled coffee and the sweat of the man.

Sebastian saw it, felt it, as one image stuttered into the next. He lost whole patches as the child's terror and tears exhausted him into sleep.

But he saw. And he knew where to begin.

Morgana opened the shop promptly at ten. Luna, her big white cat, slinked in between her feet, then settled down in the center of the room to groom her tail. Knowing the summer trade, Morgana went directly behind the counter to check the cash register. Her belly bumped gently against the glass, and she chuckled.

She was getting as big as a house. And she loved it. Loved the full, weighted sensation of carrying life. The life she and Nash had created between them.

She remembered how just that morning her husband had pressed kisses to that growing mound, then jerked back, eyes wide, as whoever was sleeping inside kicked.

"Jeez, Morgana, a foot." He'd cupped a hand over the lump, grinning. "I can practically count the toes."

As long as there's five to each foot, she thought now, and she was smiling when her door jingled open.

"Sebastian." Fresh pleasure filled her face as she held out both arms to him. "You're back."

"A couple of days ago." He took her hands, kissed them soundly, then drew back, wiggling his brows as he studied her. "My, my, aren't we huge!"

"Aren't we just?" She patted her belly as she skirted around the counter toward him.

Pregnancy hadn't dimmed her sexuality. If anything, it had enhanced it. She—as they say about brides and expectant mothers—glowed. Her fall of black, curling hair rained down the back of an unapologetically red dress that showed off excellent legs.

"I don't have to ask if you're well," he commented. "I can see that for myself."

"Then I'll ask you. I've already heard you helped clean up Chicago." She said it with a smile, but there was quiet concern in her eyes. "Was it difficult?"

"Yes. But it's done." Before he could say more, before he was certain he wanted to, a trio of customers strolled in to explore the crystals and herbs and statuary. "You're not working here alone?"

"No, Mindy will be here any minute."

"Mindy is here," her assistant announced, bounding into the shop wearing a white catsuit and a flirtatious smile for Sebastian. "Hello, handsome."

"Hi, gorgeous."

Instead of heading out of the shop, or ducking into the back room as was his habit when customers filed

in, Sebastian prowled around, fiddling restlessly with
crystals, sniffing at candles. Morgana took advantage
of the first lull to join him again.

"Looking for some magic?"

He frowned, a smooth, obsidian ball in his hand.
"I don't need visual aids."

Morgana tucked her tongue in her cheek. "Having
trouble with another spell, darling?"

Though he was very taken with it, Sebastian set the
ball down. He'd be damned if he'd give her the satisfaction. "I leave the casting to you."

"Oh, if only you would." She picked up the ball
and handed it to him. Morgana knew her cousin too
well. "Here, a gift. There's nothing like obsidian for
blocking out those bad vibrations."

He let the globe run from palm to fingertips and
back. "I suppose, being a shop owner, you'd be up
on who's who in town at the moment."

"More or less. Why?"

"What do you know about Sutherland Investigations?"

"Sutherland?" Her brow creased in thought. "It's
familiar. What is it, a detective agency?"

"Apparently."

"I think I… Mindy, didn't your boyfriend have
some business with Sutherland Investigations?"

Mindy barely glanced up from ringing a sale. "Which boyfriend?"

"The intellectual-looking one, with the hair. Insurance."

"Oh, you mean Gary." Mindy beamed at her customer. "I hope you enjoy it. Please come back. Gary's an *ex*-boyfriend," she added. "Much too possessive. Sutherland does a lot of stuff for the insurance company he works for. Gary says she's as good as they get."

"She?" Morgana glanced back at Sebastian with a cool smile. "Ah."

"There's no 'ah.'" He tweaked her nose. "I've agreed to help someone, and Sutherland is involved."

"Hmm. Is she pretty?"

"No," he said with perfect sincerity.

"Ugly, then."

"No. She's…unusual."

"The very best kind. What are you helping her with?"

"A kidnapping." The teasing light went out of his eyes. "A baby."

"Oh." Automatically she covered her own with her hands. "I'm sorry. The baby… Is the baby… Do you know?"

"He's alive. And well."

"Thank God." Even as she closed her eyes in relief, she remembered. "The baby? Is it the one who was taken from his playpen, from his own backyard, just a couple of months ago?"

"That's right."

She took his hands. "You'll find him, Sebastian. You'll find him soon."

He nodded. "I'm counting on it."

It just so happened that Mel was at that very moment in the process of typing up a bill for Underwriter's Insurance. They had her on a monthly retainer—which kept the wolf from the door—but in the previous few months she had had some additional billable expenses. She also had a fading bruise on her left shoulder where a man supposedly suffering from whiplash and slipped discs had popped her a good one when he'd discovered her taking pictures of him changing a flat tire.

A tire she had herself discreetly deflated.

Bruises aside, it had been a good week's work.

If only everything were so simple.

David. She simply couldn't get David out of her head. She knew better—had been trained better. Personal involvements meant you messed up. Thus far, she'd only proven that rule.

She'd canvassed Rose's neighborhood, questioning people who had already been interviewed by the police. And, like the police, she'd come up with three different descriptions of a car that had been parked half a block from Rose's apartment. She also had four markedly different descriptions of a "suspicious character."

The term made her smile a little. It was so detective-novel. She'd certainly learned that life was much blander than fiction. In reality, investigative work consisted of mountains of paperwork, hours of sitting in a parked car fighting boredom while you waited for something to happen, making phone call after phone call, talking to people who didn't want to talk. Or—often worse—people who talked too much and had nothing to say.

And, occasionally, there was the extra added excitement of being pushed around by a two-hundred-pound gorilla in a neck brace.

Mel wouldn't have traded it for a mountain of gold dust.

But what good was it, she wondered, what good was making a living doing what you loved, and having the talent to do a good job of it, if you couldn't help a friend? There hadn't been so many friends in her life that she could take Rose and Stan for granted.

They had given her something just by being there, by sharing David with her. The connection to family that she'd always done without.

She would have walked through fire to bring David back to them.

After tossing the billing aside, she picked up a file that hadn't been off her desk in two months. It was neatly labeled David Merrick, and its contents were miserably thin.

All his vital statistics were there—his height and weight and coloring. She had his footprints and his fingerprints. She knew his blood type and was aware of the tiny dimple on the left side of his mouth.

But the reports didn't say that the dimple deepened so sweetly when he laughed. It couldn't describe the engaging sound of that laughter, or how it felt when he pressed that soft, damp mouth to yours in a kiss. It didn't say how his pretty brown eyes sparkled when you lifted him high over your head to play airplane.

She knew how empty she felt, how sad and frightened. Just as she knew that if she multiplied those emotions by a thousand it wouldn't come close to what Rose was living with every hour of every day.

Mel opened the folder and drew out the formal studio shot of David at six months. It had been taken only a week before the kidnapping. He was grinning at the camera, his pudgy chin creased in a smile as he clutched the yellow bear she had bought for him on the day he'd come home from the hospital. His hair had begun to thicken, and it was the shade of ripening strawberries.

"We're going to find you, baby. We're going to find you and bring you home real soon. I swear it."

She put the picture away again, quickly. She had to, if she was to have any hope of proceeding in a calm and professional manner. Mooning over his picture wouldn't help David, any more than hiring a psychic with a pirate's mouth and spooky eyes would.

Oh, the man irritated her. Irritated her from the top of her head down to the soles of her feet and every possible inch between. That look on his face, that not-quite-a-smirk, not-quite-a-grin set to his mouth made her want to plant her fist there.

And his voice, smooth, with just a whisper of an Irish brogue, set her teeth on edge. There was such cool superiority in it. Except when he'd spoken to Rose, she remembered. Then it had been gentle and kind and unflaggingly patient.

Just setting her up, Mel told herself, and stepped over a pile of phone books to get to the doorway, where a refrigerator held a monstrous supply of soft drinks—all loaded with caffeine. He had just been setting Rose up, offering her hope when he had no right to.

David would be found, but he would be found by logical, meticulous police work. Not by some crackpot visionary in six-hundred-dollar boots.

She was just taking an angry swig when those boots walked through her door.

She said nothing, just continued to lean in the doorway, the bottle to her lips and her eyes shooting tiny green darts. Sebastian closed the door marked Sutherland Investigations behind him and took a lazy look around.

As offices went, he'd seen worse. And he'd certainly seen better. Her desk was army-surplus gray steel, functional and tough, but far from aesthetically pleasing. Two metal file cabinets were shoved against a wall that would have benefited from a coat of paint. There were two chairs, one in a lurid purple, the other a faded print, on either side of a skinny table that held ancient magazines and was scarred with sundry cigarette burns.

On the wall behind them, as out of place as an elegant woman in a waterfront dive, was a lovely watercolor of Monterey Bay. The room smelled inexplicably like a spring meadow.

He caught a glimpse of the room behind her and saw that it was a tiny and unbelievably disordered kitchen.

He couldn't resist.

Tucking his hands in his pockets, he smiled at her. "Some digs."

She took another drink, then dangled the bottle between two fingers. "Have you got business with me, Donovan?"

"Have you got another bottle of that?"

After a moment, she shrugged, then stepped over the phone books again to snatch one out of the refrigerator. "I don't think you came down off your mountain for a drink."

"But I rarely turn one down." He twisted off the top after she handed him the bottle. He skimmed his gaze over her, taking in the snug jeans and the scarred boots, then moving back up, to the tipped-up chin, with its fascinating little center dip, all the way to the distrustful dark green eyes. "You certainly look fetching this morning, Mary Ellen."

"Don't call me that." Though she'd meant merely to sound firm, the words gritted out between her teeth.

"Such a lovely, old-fashioned name." He tilted his head, baiting her. "Then again, I suppose Mel suits you better."

"What do you want, Donovan?"

The teasing light faded. "To find David Merrick."

She was almost fooled. Almost. The simple statement sounded so sincere, so keenly honest, that she nearly reached out. Snapping herself back, she sat on the corner of her desk and studied him.

"It's just you and me now, pal. So let's cut to the chase. You don't have any stake in this. I humored Rose because I couldn't find a way to talk her out of going to you, and because it gave her some temporary comfort. But I know your kind. Maybe you're too slick for the obvious con. You know the sort— send me twenty bucks and I'll change your life. Let me help you obtain money, power and great sex for only a small monetary contribution."

She gestured with the bottle, then drank again. "You're not the small-change sort. More the beluga and Dom Perignon type. I suppose you get your jollies by going into trances around crime scenes and spouting out clues. Maybe you even hit a few from time to time, so good for you. But you're not going to get your jollies out of Rose and Stan's unhappiness. You're not going to use their little boy as an ego boost."

He was only mildly annoyed. Sebastian assured himself that he didn't give a tinker's dam what this smart-mouthed green-eyed bimbo thought of him. The bottom line was David Merrick.

But his fingers had tightened on the bottle, and his voice, when he spoke, was entirely too soft.

"Have me all figured out, do you, Sutherland?"

"You bet your buns I do." Arrogance came off her in waves as she sat on the corner of the desk. "So let's not waste each other's time. If you feel you're owed something for hearing Rose out yesterday, bill me. I'll see you get what's coming to you."

He said nothing for a moment. It occurred to him that he'd never had the urge to throttle a woman before. Excepting his cousin Morgana. But now he imagined closing his hands around Mel's long, tanned throat. And he imagined very well.

"It's a wonder you don't stagger with that chip on your shoulder." He set the half-empty bottle down. Then, pushing impatiently through the chaos on her desk, he unearthed a pencil and a sheet of paper.

"What're you doing?" she asked when he cleared a small space and began to sketch.

"Drawing you a picture. You seem like the kind who needs visuals."

She frowned. Watching the careless way his hand streaked over the paper, she frowned deeper. She'd always envied and resented people who could draw so effortlessly. She continued to drink, telling herself she wasn't interested. But her gaze continued to be pulled back to the face emerging from the lines and curves he made.

Despite herself, she leaned closer. Somewhere in the back of her mind it registered that he smelled like horses and leather. Sleek, groomed horses, and oiled leather. The deep purple of his amethyst caught her eye. She stared at it, half-hypnotized by the way it glinted in that twist of gold on his little finger.

Artist's hands, she thought dimly. Strong and capable and elegant. She reminded herself they would probably be soft, as well—accustomed to opening champagne or undoing a lady's fancy buttons.

"I often do both at the same time."

"What?" More than a little dazed, she looked up and saw that he had stopped drawing. He was simply standing, closer than she'd realized. And watching.

"Nothing." His lips curved, but he was annoyed with himself for probing. He'd simply been curious as to why she'd been staring at his hands. "Sometimes it's best not to think too loudly." While she was chewing that over, he handed her the sketch. "This is the man who took David."

She wanted to dismiss the drawing, and the artist.

But there was something eerily right about it. Saying nothing, she walked behind her desk and opened David's folder. Inside were four police sketches. She chose one, comparing it to Sebastian's work.

His was more detailed, certainly. The witness hadn't noticed that little C-shaped scar under the left eye or the chipped front tooth. The police artist hadn't captured that expression of glittery panic. But, essentially, they were the same man—the shape of the face, the set of the eyes, the springy hair beginning to recede.

So he has a connection on the force, she told herself, trying to settle her jumping nerves. He got hold of a copy of the sketch, then embellished it a bit.

She tossed the sketch down, then settled in her chair. It squeaked rustily when she leaned back. "Why this one?"

"Because that's the one I saw. He was driving a brown Mercury. An '83 or '84. Beige interior. The back seat's ripped on the left side. He likes country music. At least that's what he had playing on the car radio when he drove off with the child. East," he murmured, and his eyes sharpened to a knife edge for just a heartbeat. "Southeast."

One of the witnesses had reported a brown car. Nondescript but unfamiliar, parked near Rose's apartment. Several days running, he'd said.

And Sebastian could have gotten that information from the police, as well, Mel reminded herself. She'd called his bluff, and he was just pushing buttons.

But if he wasn't…if there was the slightest chance…

"A face and a car." She tried to sound disinterested, but the faintest of tremors in her voice betrayed her. "No name, address and serial number?"

"You're a tough sell, Sutherland." It would be easy to dislike her, he thought, if he couldn't see—feel—how desperately she cared.

What the hell. He'd dislike her on principle.

"A child's life is at stake."

"He's safe," Sebastian said. "Safe and well cared for. A little confused, and he cries more than he did. But no one's hurt him."

She felt the breath clog up in her lungs. She wanted to believe that—that much, if nothing more.

"You're not going to talk to Rose about this," she said steadily. "It'll drive her crazy."

Ignoring her, Sebastian went on. "The man who took him was afraid. You could smell it. He took him to a woman somewhere… East." It would come. "And she dressed him in Oshkosh overalls and a red striped shirt. He was in a car seat and had a ring of plastic keys to play with. They drove most of the day, then stopped at a motel. It had a dinosaur out front. She fed him, bathed him, and when he cried she walked him until he fell asleep."

"Where?" she asked.

"Utah." He frowned a little. "Arizona, maybe, but probably Utah. The next day they drove, still southeast. She's not afraid. It's just business. They go to a mall—someplace in Texas. East Texas. It's crowded. She sits on a bench. A man sits beside her. He leaves an envelope on the bench and pushes David away in his stroller.

"The same routine the following day. David's tired of traveling and bewildered by all the strange faces. He wants home. He's taken to a house. A big stone house with old, leafy trees in the yard. South. It feels like Georgia. He's given to a woman who holds him and cries a little, and a man who holds them both. He has a room there, with blue sailboats on the wall and a mobile over the crib of circus animals. They call him Eric now."

Mel was very pale when she managed to speak. "I don't believe you."

"No, but there's a part of you that wonders if you should. Forget what you think of me, Mel. Think of David."

"I am thinking of David." She sprang to her feet,

the sketch clutched in her hand. "Give me a name, then. Give me a damn name."

"Do you think it works like that?" he tossed back. "Demand and answer? It's an art, not a pop quiz."

She let the sketch float back to the desk. "Right."

"Listen to me." He slapped his hands down on the desk, hard enough to make her jolt in reaction. "I've been in Chicago for three weeks, watching some monster slice people to ribbons in my head. Feeling his glee while he did it. Using up everything I am, everything I have, to find him before he could do it again. If I'm not working fast enough to suit you on this, Sutherland, that's too damn bad."

She backed off. Not because she was afraid of this sudden burst of temper. Because she saw something in his face, some trace of his weary horror at what he'd been through.

"Okay." She took a deep breath. "Here are the facts. I don't believe in psychics or witches or things that go bump in the night."

He had to smile. "You'll have to meet my family sometime."

"But," she continued, as if he hadn't spoken, "I'll use anything, any resource. Hell, we can use a Ouija board if it'll help get David back." She picked up the sketch again. "I've got a face. I'll start with that."

"*We'll* start with that."

Before she could come up with a suitable response, the phone rang. "Sutherland Investigations. Yeah, it's Mel. What's going down, Rico?"

Sebastian watched her attention sharpen, saw a slight smile tug at her lips. Why, she is pretty, he realized with a kind of annoyed surprise.

"Hey, babe, you can trust me." She began to write on a pad in messy, hurried scribbles. "Yeah, I know where it is. Isn't that dandy?" She listened again, nodding to herself and muttering now and then. "Come on, come on, I know the drill. I never heard of you, never saw that pretty face of yours. I'll leave your fee at O'Riley's." She paused and laughed. "In your dreams, baby."

When she hung up, Sebastian could feel the excitement shooting off her in sparks. "Take a walk, Donovan. I've got to go to work."

"I'll go with you." It was said on impulse, and almost immediately regretted. He would have taken it back if her reaction had been less scathing. She laughed again.

"Listen, pal, this isn't amateur hour. I don't need the extra baggage."

"We're going to be working together—for a hopefully brief duration. I know what I can handle,

Sutherland. I haven't got a clue about you. I'd like to see you in action."

"You want action?" She nodded slowly. "All right, hotshot. Wait here. I've got to change first."

## Chapter 3

She'd changed, all right, Sebastian thought less than ten minutes later. The woman who walked in from the back room in a pumpkin-colored leather skirt the length of a place mat was a sharp left turn away from the one who'd walked out.

Those legs were, well, just short of miraculous.

She'd done something to her face, as well. Her eyes seemed huge and heavy. Slumberous, he supposed was the word. Her mouth was dark and slick. She'd fluffled and fiddled with her hair. Now, rather than looking careless, it was tousled in a way that suggested she'd just gotten out of bed—and would be more than willing to tumble back in.

Two glittery gold balls hung from her ears, nearly touching the shoulders of a snug black tank top. Snug enough, Sebastian thought, to make any man not currently in a coma realize there was nothing beneath it but woman.

*SEX!* The word steamed into his mind in big, bold letters. This was wild, uninhibited and casually available sex.

He was certain he was about to make some snide comment, or perhaps say something rudely suggestive. But that wasn't what came out of his mouth.

"Where in the name of Finn do you think you're going dressed like that?"

Mel cocked one penciled eyebrow. "In the name of who?"

He made a dismissive gesture and tried to keep his eyes off her legs. Whatever fragrance she'd dumped all over herself made his tongue want to hang out. "You look like a—"

"Yeah." Pleased, she grinned and turned in a saucy circle. "It's my floozy look. Works like a charm. Most guys don't care if you're pretty or not if you show enough skin and cover the rest with something tight."

He shook his head. He didn't want to try to decipher that. "Why are you dressed like that?"

"Tools of the trade, Donovan." She shifted the oversize purse on her shoulder. Inside it, she carried another tool of the trade. "If you're going with me, let's hit it. I'll fill you in on the way."

It wasn't excitement he felt from her now. That she had banked. As she climbed into her car—and Lord, her skirt slithered up another inch—he caught bolts of anticipation, quicksilver streaks of fun. The kind Sebastian imagined another kind of woman might feel embarking on a shopping spree.

But Mel wasn't like any kind of woman he'd ever before encountered.

"Okay," she said as he settled into the passenger seat. "Here's the deal."

She shot away from the curb, and her driving was as quick and competent as her explanation.

There had been a rash of local robberies over the past six weeks. All electronics—televisions, VCRs, stereo equipment. A good many of the victims had been insured by Underwriter's. The police had a few leads, but nothing solid. And since no single home had been hit for more than a few hundred at a shot, it wasn't exactly number one on their hit list.

"Underwriter's is your average happy insurance

company," she commented as she winked through an amber light. "Which means they really hate to pay claims. So I've been working on it for the last few weeks."

"Your car needs a tune-up," Sebastian told her when the engine made a gagging sound.

"Yeah. Anyway, I did some poking around, and what do you know? Turns out there's a couple of guys selling TVs and such out of the back of a van. Oh, not around here. They bop over to Salinas or down to Soledad."

"How did you find out?"

She shot him a mild smile. "Legwork, Donovan. Miles and miles of legwork."

Despite his better judgment, his gaze dropped down to those long, tanned thighs. "I'll bet."

"So I've got this snitch. He's had a few unfortunate run-ins with the cops, and he's a little leery. But he kind of took to me. Because I'm private, I guess."

Sebastian coughed, cleared his throat. "Oh, yeah. I'm sure that's it."

"He's got connections," she went on. "Seeing as he did some time for B and E—breaking and entering," she explained. "And some petty larceny."

"You have fascinating friends."

"It's a good life," she said, with a laugh in her

voice. "He passes me some information, I pass him a few bills. Mostly it keeps him from picking locks. He hangs down at the docks. Strictly nontourist areas. There's a bar down there where he happened to be tossing back a few last night. Got chummy with this guy who was already soused. My friend likes a drink better if somebody else is paying for it. They got intimate in that happy way drunks do, and he finds out this guy's flush because he just hauled a load of electronic entertainment down to King City. Now, because they're the best of friends, he takes my snitch around the back of the bar to this dump of a warehouse. And what do you suppose is inside?"

"Previously owned electronics at a discount price."

Amused, she chuckled. "You catch on, Donovan."

"So why don't you just call the cops?"

"Hey, these guys might not be the James Gang, but it's a pretty good bust." Her lips were curved as she downshifted. "My bust."

"I suppose it's occurred to you that they might be...uncooperative."

When she smiled again, something hot and beautiful leapt into her eyes. "Don't worry, Donovan. I'll protect you. Now, here's what I want you to do."

When they pulled up in front of the bar a few minutes later, Sebastian had the game plan. He didn't like it, but he had it. A fastidious man, he looked dubiously at the low-slung, windowless establishment.

Seedy, he thought, but supposed that a good many bars looked seedy in the light of day. He had a feeling this one would look equally seedy in the dead of night.

It was built of cinder blocks that some enterprising soul had painted green. The paint, a particularly hideous shade, was peeling badly and showed the gray beneath, the way an old, peeling scab shows the pasty skin underneath.

It was barely noon, but there were nearly a dozen cars in the gravel lot.

Mel dropped her keys into her purse while she frowned at Sebastian. "Try to look less..."

"Human?" he suggested.

*Elegant* was the word she'd had in mind, but she'd be damned if she'd use it. "Less *Gentleman's Quarterly.* And for God's sake don't order any white wine."

"I'll restrain myself."

"Just follow the bouncing ball, Donovan, and you'll do fine."

What he followed were her swaying hips, and he wasn't sure he'd do fine at all.

The smell of the place assaulted him the moment Mel pulled open the door. Stale smoke, stale beer, stale sweat. There was a rumbling sound from the jukebox, and, though Sebastian had very eclectic tastes in music, he hoped he wouldn't be subjected to that surly sound for long.

Men were lined up at the bar—the kind of men with burly forearms littered with tattoos. This particular artwork ran heavily in favor of snakes and skulls. There was a clatter as four oily-looking characters shot nine ball. Some glanced up, their gazes sliding over Sebastian with a kind of smirking derision and lingering on Mel, longer and with more affection.

He picked up on scattered thoughts—easy enough, since the average IQ of the patrons hovered below three digits. His lips twitched once. He hadn't realized there were so many ways to describe a... lady.

The lady in question, one of three currently enjoying the atmosphere, sauntered up to the bar and wiggled her leather-clad bottom onto a stool. That wide, slicked mouth was pursed in a sexy pout. "Least you can do is buy me a beer," she said to Sebastian in a breathy little voice that caught him off guard. Her eyes narrowed briefly in warning, and he remembered his cue.

"Listen, sweetcakes, I told you it wasn't my fault."

*Sweetcakes?* Mel stopped herself from rolling her eyes. "Sure, nothing is. You get canned, it's not your fault. You lose a hundred bucks playing poker with your slimy friends, it's not your fault. Give me a beer, will you?" she called to the bartender, and crossed those long, lovely legs.

Trying to hulk a bit, Sebastian held up two fingers, then slid onto the stool beside her. "I told you... Didn't I tell you that creep had it in for me at work? And why don't you get off my back?"

"Oh, sure." She sniffed as the beers were slapped down in front of them. When Sebastian reached for his back pocket, it occurred to her that his wallet was probably worth more than the combined liquid assets of the bar's patrons. And that it was likely filled with plenty of the green stuff, along with a few flashy gold credit cards.

She hissed at him.

He understood instantly, and that would give her some food for thought later. His hand hesitated, then dropped away.

"Tapped out again?" she said, a sneer in her voice. "Isn't that just swell?" With obvious reluctance, she dug into her bag and unearthed two ragged dollar bills. "You're such a loser, Harry."

*Harry?* Sebastian's frown was entirely authentic. "I'll have some coming in. I got ten on the game."

"Oh, sure, sure. You'll be rolling in it." She gave him her back and, sipping at the mug of beer, scanned the room.

She had Rico's description. It took her less than two minutes to zero in on the man Rico's pal had called Eddie. Eddie was a real fun guy, according to Rico's drinking partner. He was the day man, the one who doled out the merchandise for transport and sale. And, according to Rico, he had a real soft spot for the ladies.

Mel swung her leg in time with the music and made sure she caught Eddie's eye. She smiled, fluttered, and sent out conflicting signals.

To Eddie her smile said: Hey there, big guy. I've been looking for someone just like you all my life.

To Sebastian, who had tuned in to her just enough to keep her from surprising him, it was: Fat, hairless jerk.

He turned and took a look for himself. Hairless, true, Sebastian thought. But it wasn't all fat stuffed into that sleeveless T-shirt. There was plenty of muscle mixed in.

"Listen, honey." Sebastian put a hand on Mel's shoulder and had it shrugged off.

"I'm tired of excuses, Harry. Sick and damn tired.

They're all just a crock. You got no money. You lose all of mine. You can't even put fifty together to get the TV fixed. And you know how much I like my shows."

"You watch the tube too much, anyway."

"Oh, fine." She was fired up now, and she swung around to face him. "I work my butt off waiting tables half the night, and you give me grief because I like to sit down, put my feet up and watch a little TV. It don't cost nothing to watch."

"It's going to cost fifty bucks."

She shoved him, sliding off the stool as she did. "You just lost twice that in a damn card game, and some of it was mine."

"I said get off my back." He was getting into it now, almost enjoying it. Maybe it was because he remembered he'd been instructed to push her around a little. "Whine and bitch, that's all you do." He grabbed her, trying to make a good show of it. Her head fell back and her eyes were bright with defiance. That...sexy? Oh, yes, very sexy—mouth moved into a pout, and he had to struggle to stay in character.

She saw something in his eyes, very briefly, very powerfully. Mel's heart tripped right up to her throat and beat there like a big bass drum.

"I don't have to take this crap from you." He gave

her a good shake, as much to settle himself as for effect. "If you don't like the way things are, you can try the door."

"You better take your hands off me." She made her voice tremble. It was embarrassing, but necessary. "I told you what would happen if you ever hit me again."

Hit her? Good Lord! "Just get your butt outside, Crystal." He started to push her toward the door and found his face pressed against a beefy chest covered in a sweaty T-shirt that announced that its owner was A Hard Driving Man.

"The little lady wants hands off, jerkface."

Sebastian looked up into Eddie's wide smile. Mel was sniffling beside him, really laying it on. Hoping for more even ground, Sebastian rose from the stool so that he and the knight errant were eye-to-eye.

"Mind your own business."

Eddie knocked him back on the stool with one blow. Sebastian was certain he was going to feel the imprint of the heel of that sledgehammer hand on his chest for years to come.

"You want I should take him out and mess him up, sweetheart?"

Mel dried her lashes and seemed to consider it. She hesitated just long enough to make Sebastian sweat. "No." She laid a trembling hand on Eddie's arm. "He ain't worth it." Fluttering, she turned her admiring face up to his. "You're awfully nice. There're hardly any gentlemen left in this world a girl can count on."

"Why don't you come on and sit down at my table?" He put a tree-trunk arm around her waist. "I'll buy you a drink and you can take a load off."

"That's real sweet."

She sauntered off with him. Wanting to put on a good show, Sebastian made as if to follow them. One of the contestants at the pool table grinned and slapped a cue on his palm. Suitably warned, Sebastian skulked down to the end of the bar and nursed his beer.

She made him wait an hour and a half. He couldn't even order a second beer without breaking his cover and was enduring nasty looks from the bartender as he nibbled on peanuts and made the last half inch of his drink last forever.

He'd just about had it. His idea of a good time was not sitting in a smelly bar watching some sumo wrestler paw the woman he'd come with. Even if he didn't have any emotional investment. And even, he thought darkly, if that woman giggled with every appearance of enjoyment every time one of those ham-sized hands rubbed her leg.

It would serve her right if he just strolled out, caught himself a cab and left her to it.

In Mel's opinion, everything was going just fine. Fine and dandy. Sir Eddie, as she called him—much to his delight—was getting slowly and steadily drunk. Not pie-eyed, just nice and vulnerable. And he was doing plenty of talking. Men just loved to brag to an eager woman—especially when they were juiced.

He'd just come into a nice chunk of change, so Eddie said. And maybe she'd like to help him spend a little of it.

She'd love to. Of course, she had to get to work in a couple of hours, and she didn't finish her shift until one, but after that...

When she had him softened up, she gave him a sob story. How she and Harry had been together for almost six whole months. How he ran through money like water and kept her from having a good time. She didn't ask for much. Just some pretty clothes and a few laughs. And now it was really bad, just plain awful, because her TV had broken down. Here she'd been saving up for a VCR so she could tape shows while she worked, and now the TV was on the fritz. Worse, Harry had blown his money and hers on cards, so now she didn't even have the fifty to fix the set.

"I really like to watch, you know?" She toyed with her second beer. Eddie was working on number seven. "In the afternoon they got these shows, and all the women have these pretty clothes. Then they switch me to the day shift and I miss out. I can never catch up with what's happening. And you know…" She leaned forward, confidentially, so that her breasts rubbed against his forearm. "They got these love scenes on them. Watching them just gets me so… hot."

Eddie watched her tongue peek out and run around her lips. He plainly thought he'd died and gone to heaven. "I guess it's not much fun watching something like that all alone."

"Be more fun with somebody." She gave him a look that told him he was the only possible somebody. "If I had a set that worked, it might be nice. I like daytime, you know. When everybody else is working or shopping, and you can be…in bed." Sighing, she ran her fingertip around her mug.

"It's daytime now."

"Yeah. But I haven't got a TV." She giggled, as if it were a great joke.

"I might be able to help you with that, baby."

She let her eyes widen, then brought her lashes coyly down. "Aw, gee, that's really sweet of you, Eddie.

I couldn't let you give me the fifty. It wouldn't be right."

"What do you want to toss money at an old set for, anyway? You can have a new one."

"Oh, yeah." She snorted into her beer. "And I could have me a diamond tiara, too."

"Can't help you on that, but I can get you a set."

"Come on." She shot him a disbelieving look and let her hand rest on his knee. "How?"

He puffed out his massive chest. "Just so happens, I'm in the business."

"You sell TVs?" She cocked her head and had her eyes blinking in fascination. "You're pulling my leg."

"Not now." He winked. "Maybe later."

Mel laughed heartily. "Oh, you're a card, Sir Eddie." She drank again, sighed again. "I wish you weren't fooling. If you could get me one, I'd be awfully grateful."

He leaned closer. She could smell the beer and smoke on his breath. "How grateful?"

Mel wiggled toward him, put her mouth to his ear and whispered a suggestion that would have made the worldly Sebastian stutter.

Short of breath, Eddie finished off his beer in one gulp and grabbed her hand. "Come on, sweet thing. I got something to show you."

Mel went along, not bothering to glance in Sebastian's direction. She sincerely hoped that what Eddie was about to show her was a television.

"Where're we going?" she asked as he led her to the back of the building.

"My office, babe." A sly wink. "Me and my partners got a little business back here."

He took her over a rubble of broken bottles, trash and piles of gravel to another concrete building, perhaps half the size of the bar. After three raps on the door, it was opened by a skinny man of about twenty wearing horn-rims and carrying a clipboard.

"What's the deal, Eddie?"

"The lady needs a TV." He swung his arm over Mel's shoulder and squeezed. "Crystal, honey, this is Bobby."

"'Meetcha," Bobby said with a bounce of his head. "Look, Eddie, I don't think this is a good idea. Frank's going to be mad as hell."

"Hey, I got as much right as Frank." Eddie bulled his way in.

Ah, Mel thought, and sighed. For real.

The fluorescent bulbs overhead shone down on the blank single eyes of more than a dozen televisions. They sat cheek by jowl with CD players, VCRs, stereo systems. Tossed in for good measure were several boom boxes, personal computers, tele-

phone answering machines, and one lonely micro-
wave oven.

"Wow!" She clapped her hands together. "Oh,
wow, Eddie! Look at all this! It's like a regular department store."

Full of confidence, and swaying only a little, Eddie
winked at the nervous Bobby. "We're what you call
suppliers. We don't do any retail out of here. This is
just like our warehouse. Go ahead, look around."

Still playing her role, Mel walked over to the televisions, running her hands over their screens as if her
fingers were walking in mink.

"Frank's not going to like this," Bobby hissed.

"So what he don't know he don't have to not like.
Right, Bobby?"

Bobby, who was outweighed by a hundred pounds,
nodded. "Sure, Eddie. But bringing a broad in
here—"

"She's okay. Great legs, but not much brains. I'm
going to give her a set—and then I'm going to get
lucky." He moved past Eddie to join Mel. "See one
you like, baby?"

"Oh, they're great. Really great. Do you mean I
can really have one? Just pick one out and have it?"

"Why, sure." He gave her a quick, intimate
squeeze. "We got this breakage insurance. So I'll just

have old Bobby there put down like one got busted. That's all there is to it."

"Really?" She tossed her head, moving just far enough out of reach that she could easily slip a hand into her bag. "That's great, Eddie. But it looks to me like you're the one who's busted."

She pulled out a nickel-plated .38.

"A cop!" Bobby nearly screeched the words, while Eddie's face settled into a thoughtful frown. "Jeez, Eddie, she's a cop!"

"There you go. Don't," she warned as Bobby edged to the door. "Just have a scat, Bobby. On the floor there. And sit on your hands, will you?"

"You bitch," Eddie said, in a considering voice that put Mel on guard. "I should've smelled cop."

"I'm private," she told him. "That might be the reason." She gestured with the gun. "Let's take it outside, Eddie."

"No woman's going to double-cross me—gun or no gun."

He lunged.

She didn't want to shoot him. She really didn't. He wasn't anything more than a fat, second-rate thief, and he didn't deserve a bullet. Instead, she twisted, veering left and counting on her speed and agility and his beer-induced sluggishness.

He missed and rammed headlong into a twenty-five inch screen. Mel wasn't sure who was the victor, but the screen cracked like an egg, and Eddie went down hard.

There was a sound behind her. When she whirled she had time to see Sebastian wrap an arm around Bobby's throat. One quick squeeze had him dropping the hammer he'd been lifting over Mel's head.

"It probably wouldn't have made a dent," Sebastian said between his teeth as Bobby crumpled bonelessly to the concrete floor. "You didn't tell me you had a gun."

"I didn't think I had to. You're supposed to be psychic."

Sebastian picked up the hammer, tapping it gently against his palm. "Keep it up, Sutherland."

She merely shrugged and took another look at the loot. "Nice haul. Why don't you go call the cops? I'll keep an eye on these two."

"Fine." He was sure it was too much to expect her to thank him for saving her from a concussion, or worse. The best he could do was slam the door behind him.

It was nearly an hour later when Sebastian stood by and watched Mel sitting on the hood of her car.

She was going over the fine details with what appeared to be a very disgruntled detective.

Haverman, Sebastian remembered. He'd run into him once or twice.

Then he dismissed the cop and concentrated on Mel.

She'd pulled off the earrings and was still rubbing her lobes from time to time. Most of the goo on her face had been wiped off with tissue. Her unpainted mouth and naturally flushed cheeks made a devastating contrast with the big, heavy-lidded eyes.

Pretty? Had he granted her pretty? Sebastian wondered. Hell, she was gorgeous. In the right light, at the right angle, she was drop-dead gorgeous. Then she might turn and be merely mildly attractive again.

That held an odd and disturbing sort of magic.

But he didn't care how she looked, he reminded himself. He didn't care, because he was plenty peeved. She'd dragged him into this. It didn't matter that he'd volunteered to come along. Once he had, she'd set the rules, and he'd had plenty of time to decide he didn't like them.

She'd gone alone into that storage building with a man built like two fullbacks. And she'd had a gun. No little peashooter, either, but a regular cannon.

What the hell would she have done if she'd had to

use it? Or—Lord—if that mountain of betrayed lust had gotten it away from her?

"Look," Mel was saying to Haverman. "You've got your sources, I've got mine. I got a tip. I followed it up." She was moving her shoulders carelessly, but, oh, she was enjoying this. "You've got no beef with me, Lieutenant."

"I want to know who put you on to this, Sutherland." It was a matter of principle for him. He was a cop, after all, a *real* cop. Not only was she a PI, she was a female PI. It just plain grated on him.

"And I don't have to tell you." Then her lips quirked, because the idea was so beautiful, so inspired. "But, since we're pals, I'll clue you in." She jerked her thumb toward Sebastian. "He did."

"Sutherland…" Sebastian began.

"Come on, Donovan, what does it hurt?" This time she smiled and brought him in on the joke. "This is Lieutenant Haverman."

"We've met."

"Sure." Now Haverman was not only piqued but deflated. Women PIs and psychics. What was law enforcement coming to? "I didn't think missing TVs was your gig."

"A vision's a vision," Sebastian said complacently, and had Mel hooting.

"So how come you passed it to her?" It didn't sit right with him. "You always come to the cops."

"Yeah." Sebastian shot a glittering look at Mel over his shoulder. "But she's got better legs."

Mel laughed so hard she nearly fell off the car. Haverman grumbled a little more and then stalked off. After all, he thought, he had two suspects in hand—and if he tried to shake Donovan, he'd have the chief on his case.

"Good going, slick." Still chuckling, Mel gave Sebastian a friendly bop on the shoulder. "I didn't think you had it in you."

He merely lifted a brow. "There are a great many things you might be surprised I have in me."

"Yeah, right." She twisted her head to watch Haverman climb in his car. "The lieutenant's not such a bad guy. He just figures PIs belong in the pages of a book, and women belong one step away from the oven." Because the sun was warm and the deed had been done well, she was content to sit on the car for few minutes and enjoy the small triumph. "You did good…Harry."

"Thanks, Crystal," he said, and tried not to let his lips twitch into a smile. "Now, I'd appreciate it if next time you filled me in on the entire plan before we start."

"Oh, I don't think there's a next time coming soon. But this was fun."

"Fun." He said the word slowly, understanding that that was precisely what she meant. "You really enjoyed it. Dressing up like a tart, making a scene, having that muscle-bound throwback drool on you."

She offered a bland smile. "I'm entitled to some on-the-job benefits, aren't I?"

"And it was fun, I suppose, to nearly have your head cracked open?"

"Nearly's the key." Feeling more kindly toward him, she patted his arm. "Come on, Donovan, loosen up. I said you did good."

"That, I take it, is your way of thanking me for saving your thick skull."

"Hey, I could've handled Bobby fine, but I appreciate the backup. Okay?"

"No." He slapped his hands down on the hood on either side of her hips. "It is not okay. If this is a taste of how you do business, you and I are going to set some rules."

"I've got rules. My rules." His eyes were the color of smoke now, she thought. Not the kind that had hung listlessly at the ceiling of the bar, but the sort that plumes up into the night from a crackling good bonfire. "Now back off, Donovan."

*Make me.* He hated—no, detested—the fact that the childish, taunting phrase was the first thing to pop into his head. He wasn't a child. And neither was she—sitting there, daring him with that insolent lift to her chin and that half smirk on her beautiful mouth.

His right hand fisted. It was tempting to give her one good pop on that damnably arrogant chin. But her mouth seemed a better notion. And he had a much more satisfying idea about what could be done with it.

He snatched her off the hood of the car so quickly that she didn't think to use any of the defensive countermoves that were second nature to her. She was still blinking when his arms came around her, when one hand cupped firmly on the back of her head, fingers spread.

"What the hell do you think—?"

That was it. The words clicked off as completely as her brain the moment his mouth clamped over hers. She didn't break away or shift her body to one side to toss him over her shoulder. She didn't bring her knee up in a way that would have had him dropping to his and gasping. She simply stood there and let his lips grind her mind to mush.

He was sorry she'd pushed him beyond his own rules. Grabbing unwilling women was not on Sebas-

tian's list of things to do. And he was sorry—desperately sorry, because she didn't taste the way he'd
been certain she would. A woman with a personality
like Mel's should have had a vinegary flavor. She
should have tasted prickly and tart.

Oh, but she was sweet.

It wasn't sugar he thought of, or the kind of gooey
candy that came wrapped in gold foil. It was honey,
rich, thick, wild honey that you were compelled to
lick off your finger. The kind that, even as a child,
he'd never been able to resist.

When her lips opened for his, he dived in.
Wanting more.

His hands weren't soft. That was the first wayward
thought that stumbled into her brain. They were hard
and strong and just a little rough. She could feel those
fingers pressed against the back of her neck. The
skin there seemed to be on fire.

He pulled her closer, so that their bodies made
one long shadow on the littered gravel. As sensations
swarmed through her system, she threw her arms
around him and gave him back desire for desire.

It was different now. She thought she heard him
curse before he changed the angle of the kiss, his
teeth scraping over her lips and nearly making her cry
out from the bolt of pleasure. Her heart was beating

in her head, echoing in her ears like a train picking up speed in a tunnel.

It would break through any moment, break out of the dark and into the light, and then she would—

"Hey!"

The shout didn't even register. The movement of Sebastian's lips on hers did, a movement that was at first her name, and then another oath.

"Hey!"

Sebastian heard the shout, and the crunch of footsteps on gravel. He could cheerfully have committed murder. He kept one arm around Mel's waist and his hand firm on her neck as he turned his head and stared into a grizzled face under a Dodgers baseball cap.

"Go away." The order was close to a snarl. "Go very far away."

"Listen, bud, I just wanna know how come the bar's closed."

"They ran out of vodka." He could already feel Mel retreating from him, and would have sworn again if it would have done any good.

"Well, hell, all I want's a lousy beer." Having successfully destroyed the mood, the Dodgers fan clumped back to his pickup and drove off.

Mel had crossed her arms over her breasts and

was cupping her elbows as if she were warding off a brisk wind.

"Mary Ellen…" Sebastian began.

"Don't call me that." Staggered, she jerked back and came up hard against her car.

Her lips were vibrating. She wanted to press her hand against them to make it stop, but she didn't dare. Her pulse was beating in her throat in a quick, jumpy rhythm. She wanted that to stop, too, to slow and even out until it was normal and as it should be.

God. Good God. She'd been all over him, practically climbing on him. Letting him touch her.

He wasn't touching her now, but he looked like he might. Pride prevented her from shifting away, but she braced, ready to block another assault on her senses.

"Why did you do that?"

He resisted the urge to dip in and see what she was really feeling, to compare it to what was going on inside him. But he'd already taken unfair advantage. "I haven't the vaguest idea."

"Well, don't get any more ideas." She was surprised that his answer hurt. What had she expected? she asked herself. Did she think he might have said he'd been unable to resist her? That he'd been overwhelmed with passion? She lifted her chin.

"I can handle being pawed on the job, but not on my own time. Clear?"

His eyes flashed—once. Then, with more restraint than she could have imagined, he lifted his hands, palms out. "Clear," he repeated. "Hands off."

"All right, then." She wasn't going to make a big deal out of it, she decided as she dug in her bag for her keys. It was over. And it hadn't meant a thing to either of them. "I've got to get back, make some calls." When he took a step forward, her head snapped up, as if she were a deer scenting a wolf.

"I'm just opening your door," Sebastian said, though he discovered he wasn't the least bit displeased by her reaction.

"Thanks." She climbed in and slammed it herself. She had to clear her throat to be certain her voice would be careless. "Climb aboard, Donovan. I've got places to go."

"Question," he said after he slipped in beside her. "Do you eat?"

"Mostly when I'm hungry. Why?"

There was a wariness in her eyes that he was enjoying a great deal. "Seeing as all I've had since this morning was bar nuts, I was thinking late lunch, early dinner. Why don't you stop off somewhere? I'll buy you a burger."

She frowned over that for a moment, poking the suggestion for pitfalls. "I could use a burger," she decided. "But we'll go dutch."

He smiled and settled back in his seat. "Whatever you say, Sutherland."

*Chapter 4*

Mel spent most of the morning doing door-to-doors in Rose's neighborhood with Sebastian's sketch in her hand. By that afternoon, the score was three positive IDs, four offers of coffee and one lewd proposition.

One of the positive IDs also corroborated Sebastian's description of the car, right down to the dented door. And that gave Mel a very uncomfortable feeling.

It didn't stop her from backtracking. There was a name on her list that continued to nag at her. Mel had a hunch Mrs. O'Dell in apartment 317 knew more than she was saying.

For the second time that day Mel knocked on the dull brown door, wiped her feet on the grass-green welcome mat with the white daisy in the corner. From inside she could hear the whining of children and the bright applause of a television game show.

As it had before, the door opened a few inches, and Mel looked down into the chocolate-smeared face of a young boy. "Hi. Is your mom home?"

"She don't let me say to strangers."

"Right. Maybe you could go get her."

Bumping a sneakered foot against the doorjamb, the boy seemed to consider. "If I had a gun, I could shoot you."

"Then it looks like this is my lucky day." She crouched down until they were eye-to-eye. "Chocolate pudding, right?" she said, studying the smears around his mouth. "Did you get that from licking the spoon after your mom made it?"

"Yeah." He shifted his feet and began to eye her with more interest. "How'd you know that?"

"Elementary, my dear puddingface. The smears are pretty fresh, and it's too close to lunch for your mom to let you have a whole bowl."

The boy tilted his head. "Maybe I snuck it."

"Maybe," Mel agreed. "But then you'd be pretty dumb not to wash off the evidence."

He started to grin when his mother swooped down from behind. "Billy! Didn't I tell you not to answer the door?" She hauled him back one-handed. The other arm was full of a wiggling girl with teary eyes. Mrs. O'Dell sent Mel one impatient look. "What are you doing back around here? I told you everything I could already."

"You were a big help, Mrs. O'Dell. It's my fault, really. I'm just trying to put everything in order," Mel continued, slipping into the cluttered living room as she spoke. "I hate to bother you again, especially since you were so helpful before."

Mel almost choked on that. Mrs. O'Dell had been suspicious, unfriendly and curt. Just, Mel thought as she warmed up her apologetic smile, as the lady was going to be now.

"I looked at your picture." Mrs. O'Dell jiggled her daughter on her hip. "I told you everything I know. Just like I told the police."

"I know. And I'm sure it's inconvenient to have your busy day constantly interrupted." Mel stepped over a platoon of G.I. Joes that had been overrun by a miniature fire truck. "But you see, your living room windows look right down on where the perpetrator was allegedly parked."

Mrs. O'Dell set her daughter down, and the little girl toddled toward the TV and sat down hard on her diapered bottom. "So?"

"Well, I couldn't help but notice how clean your windows are. The cleanest ones in the entire building. You know, if you look up here from down on the street, they shine like diamonds."

The flattery smoothed away Mrs. O'Dell's frown. "I take pride in my home. I don't mind clutter—with two kids you're going to have plenty of that. But I don't tolerate dirt."

"Yes, ma'am. It seems to me that to have windows looking like that you'd have to keep after them."

"You're telling me. Living this close to the water, you get that salt scum." With a mother's radar, she shot a look over her shoulder. "Billy, don't let the baby put those dirty soldiers in her mouth. Give her your truck."

"But, Mom…"

"Just for a little while." Satisfied that she would be obeyed, Mrs. O'Dell glanced back. "Where was I?"

"Salt scum," Mel prompted.

"Sure. And the dust and dirt that comes from having cars going up and down the road. Fingerprints." She nearly smiled. "Seems I'm always chasing somebody's fingerprints."

Yeah, Mel thought. Me too.

"I know it must take a lot of work to keep your place up like this, raising two kids."

"Not everyone thinks so. Some people figure if you don't carry a briefcase and commute to some office every day you're not working."

"I've always thought holding together a home and family is the most important career there is."

Mrs. O'Dell took the dust rag that was hanging out of the back pocket of her shorts and rubbed at the surface of a table. "Well."

"And the windows," Mel said, gently leading her back. "I was wondering how often you have to wash them."

"Every month, like clockwork."

"You'd have a real good view of the neighborhood."

"I don't have time to spy on my neighbors."

"No, ma'am. But you might notice things, casually."

"Well, I'm not blind. I saw that man hanging around. I told you that."

"Yes, you did. I was thinking, if you happened to be washing the windows, you might have noticed him down there. I imagine it would take you about an hour to do the job…"

"Forty-five minutes."

"Uh-huh. Well, if he was down there that long,

sitting in his car, it would have struck you as unusual, wouldn't it?"

"He got out and walked around."

"Oh?" Mel wondered if she dared take out her notepad. Better to talk now and write it all down later, she decided.

"Both days," Mrs. O'Dell added.

"Both days?"

"The day I did the windows, and the day I washed the curtains. I really didn't think anything of it. I don't poke around into other people's business."

"No, I'm sure you don't." But I do, Mel thought, her heart hammering. I do. And I just need a little more. "Do you remember which days you noticed him?"

"Did the windows the first of the month, like always. A couple days later, I noticed the curtains were looking a little dingy, so I took them down and washed them. Saw him across the street then, walking down the sidewalk."

"David Merrick was taken on the fourth of May."

Mrs. O'Dell frowned again, then glanced at her children. When she was satisfied they were squabbling and not paying any attention, she nodded. "I know. And, like I told you before, it just breaks my heart. A little baby like that, stolen practically out of his mother's arms. I haven't let Billy go out alone all summer."

Mel laid a hand on her arm to make a connection, woman to woman. "You don't have to know Rose Merrick to understand what she's going through. You're a mother."

It got through to her. Mel could see it in the way moisture sprang to Mrs. O'Dell's eyes. "I wish I could help. I just didn't see anything more than that. All I remember is thinking that this neighborhood should be safe. That you shouldn't have to be afraid to let your children walk across the street to play with a friend. You shouldn't have to worry every day that someone's going to come back and pick out your child and drive away with him."

"No, you shouldn't. Rose and Stan Merrick shouldn't be wondering if they'll ever see their son again. Someone drove away with David, Mrs. O'Dell. Someone who was parked right under your window. Maybe you weren't paying attention at the time, but if you'd clear your mind for a minute and think back… You might have noticed his car, some little thing about his car."

"That beat-up old thing? I didn't pay any mind to it."

"It was black? Red?"

Mrs. O'Dell shrugged. "Dirty is what it was. Might have been brown. Might have been green, under all that grime."

Mel took a leap of faith. "Out-of-state plates, I imagine."

After a moment's consideration, Mrs. O'Dell shook her head. "Nope. I guess I might have wondered why he was just sitting down there. Sometimes your mind wanders when you're working, and I was thinking he might have been visiting someone, waiting for them to get home. Then I was figuring he hadn't come all that far 'cause he had state plates."

Mel banked down her excitement and mentally crossed her fingers. "I always used to play this game when I was a kid. My mom and I traveled a lot, and she tried to give me things to do. I guess you know how car trips are with kids."

Mrs. O'Dell rolled her eyes. For the first time, there was a trace of humor in them. "Oh, do I."

"I always tried to make words out of the letters on plates. Or come up with funny names for what the initials stood for."

"We do the same thing with Billy. He's old enough. But the baby…"

"Maybe you noticed the license number, casually, while you were working. Without even thinking about it, if you know what I mean."

And Mel could see that she did try for a minute. Her lips pursed, her eyes narrowed. Then she made an impatient movement with her dust rag and closed down. "I've got a lot of more important things on my mind. I saw it was a California plate, like I said, but I didn't stand there and play games with it."

"No, of course not, but sometimes you pick up things without even knowing it. Then, when you think back—"

"Miss—"

"Sutherland," Mel told her.

"I'd like to help you. Really. My heart goes out to that poor woman and her husband. But I make a habit of minding my own business and keeping to my own. Now there's nothing else I can tell you, and I'm falling behind schedule."

Recognizing the wall she'd just hit, Mel took out a business card. "If you remember anything about the plate, anything at all, would you call me?"

Billy piped up. "Said cat."

"Billy, don't interrupt when people are talking."

He shrugged and drove his fire truck up his sister's leg to make her giggle.

"What said cat?" Mel asked.

"The car did." Billy made engine noises. "*K-a-t,* that spells *cat,*" he chanted, and had his mother sighing.

"You don't spell *cat* with a k. It's *c-a-t.* I can't believe you'll be going into the second grade and—"

Mel put a hand on Mrs. O'Dell's arm. "Please," she murmured, then squatted down in front of Billy. "Did you see the car down there Billy, the dirty brown car?"

"Sure. When I came home from school it was there. Freddy's mom had the pool."

"Car pool," Mrs. O'Dell said quietly.

"She let me off right behind it. I don't like riding with Freddy, 'cause he pinches."

"Did you play the license plate game with the brown car?" Mel asked.

"I like it when they make words. Like *cat.*"

"You're sure it was that brown car? Not some other car you saw on the drive home from school?"

"No, 'cause it was parked just out front the whole week Freddy's mom drove me. Sometimes it was on the other side of the street. Then it wasn't there anymore when Mom had the pool."

"Do you remember the numbers, Billy?"

"I don't like numbers. Letters are better. *K-a-t,*" he repeated. Then he looked up at his mother. "If it doesn't spell *cat,* what does it spell?"

With a grin, Mel kissed him right on the chocolate-smeared mouth. "This time it spells *thanks.* Thanks a lot."

Mel was practically singing when she walked back into Sutherland Investigations. She had something.

Maybe it was only half of a license plate, and maybe the information had come from a six-year-old, but she had something.

She switched her answering machine to playback, then nipped into the kitchen for a soft drink. Her self-satisfied smile remained as she jotted down the messages.

Good solid investigative work, she told herself. That was the way you got things done. Persistence didn't hurt. She didn't imagine the police had managed to get anywhere near Billy O'Dell, or that they would have considered him a viable witness.

Solid investigative work, persistence—and hunches. Mel believed in hunches, just as she believed they were part of an investigator's makeup. But that was a far cry from psychic visions.

Her smile tilted toward a smirk as she thought of Sebastian. Maybe he had gotten lucky with the sketch and the car. But maybe it was just as she'd thought before. A connection on the force could have given him that data.

She wouldn't mind rubbing his nose in this new information.

Not that he was all bad, she thought, feeling charitable. He'd been okay when they'd shared a burger the evening before. No more come-ons—which she'd been positive she would have nipped in the bud. And he hadn't gotten spooky on her, either.

Actually, she remembered, they'd talked. Mostly books and movies, those old conversational standbys. But he had been interesting. When he wasn't irritating her, his voice was rather pleasant, with that whisper of a brogue.

A brogue that had deepened when he'd murmured to her, his lips sliding over hers.

Annoyed, she shook herself. She wasn't going to think about that. She'd been kissed before, and she wasn't against the practice. She simply preferred to choose her own time and place.

And if she hadn't had a reaction quite like that before, it was because he'd taken her so completely by surprise.

That wouldn't happen again, either.

In fact, the way things were going, she wasn't going to need Sebastian Donovan and his hocus-pocus any longer. She had a few contacts at the Department of Motor Vehicles, and once she called in with the partial plate she would...

Her thoughts trailed off as Sebastian's voice flowed out of her answering machine.

"Ah, Sutherland, sorry I missed you. Out sleuthing, I suppose."

She made a face at the machine. An immature reaction, she readily admitted. But the laughter in his voice demanded it.

"I thought you might be interested in some new information. I've been working on the car. The left rear tire's nearly bald—which could give our man a great deal of trouble, since his spare is flat."

"Give me a break, Donovan," she muttered. She rose, deciding to turn off the machine, and the voice.

"Oh, by the way, the car has California plates. KAT 2544."

Mel's mouth fell open as her finger hesitated on the button.

"I thought you might be able to work your detective magic with that tidbit. Let me know what you come up with, won't you, love? I'll be home this evening. Good hunting, Mary Ellen."

"Son of a—" She gritted her teeth and switched the machine off.

She didn't like it. She didn't like it one damn bit, but she downshifted and started up the narrow, bumpy lane to Sebastian's house. Not for a minute did she believe he'd dreamed the plate number—or whatever term he would use—but, since he'd given her the tip, she felt obliged to do a follow-up.

When she reached the top of his lane, she was torn between elation at the progress she'd made and irritation at having to deal with him again. She'd be professional, she promised herself as she pulled between a muscular-looking Harley and a late-model minivan.

After climbing the steps, she gave a brisk knock on the door. The knocker she used was a brass figure of a snarling wolf. Intrigued, Mel played with it for a moment while she waited. When there was no response, Mel did what came naturally. She peeked in the windows.

She saw no one, only the lofty living room on one side and a very impressive library on the other. If her conscience had allowed, she would have turned away and gone home. But to do so would be both cowardly and petty. Instead, she went back down the steps and started around the house.

Mel spotted him standing inside a paddock, his arm intimately around a slim blonde in snug jeans. They were laughing, and the sound they made together was as intimate as their stance.

The quick bolt of heat baffled her. She didn't give a hang if he had a lady. She didn't care if he had a bloody harem. This was business.

But the fact that he would kiss a woman senseless

one day and be snuggled up to another the next told
Mel just what kind of a man Sebastian Donovan was.

A creep.

Despite it, she would be professional. Digging her
hands into her pockets, she strode across the lawn
toward the weathered fence.

"Hey, Donovan."

They both turned, man and woman. Mel could see
that the female was not only slim and blond, but lovely,
too. Absolutely lovely, with calm gray eyes and a soft,
full mouth that was already curved in a half smile.

Mel felt like a big mongrel dog faced with a glossy
purebred.

As she scowled, Mel saw him murmur something
to the woman, kiss her smooth temple, then come
over to lean against the fence.

"How you doing, Sutherland?"

"I got your message."

"I assumed you did. Ana, this is Mel Sutherland,
a private investigator. Mel, Anastasia Donovan. My
cousin."

"It's nice to meet you." Ana held out a hand as
Mel approached the fence. "Sebastian's told me
about the case you're working on. I hope you find
the child quickly."

"Thanks." Mel accepted the hand. There was

something so soothing about the voice, about the touch, that she felt half of her tension dissolve. "I'm making some progress."

"The boy's parents must be frantic."

"They're scared, but they're holding up."

"I'm sure it helps them, having someone who cares so much trying to help."

Anastasia stepped back, wishing she could do something to help. But, like Sebastian, she had learned she couldn't be all things to all people.

"I'm sure you have business," she continued.

"I don't want to interrupt." Mel flicked a glance at Sebastian, then looked over his shoulder to where the horses stood. The quick pleasure showed in her face before she looked away again. "I only need a minute."

"No, take your time." Graceful as a doe, Ana vaulted over the fence. "I was just leaving. Will you make the movies tomorrow night, Sebastian?"

"Whose turn is it?"

"It's Morgana's. She said she felt like murder, so we're going to see a thriller."

"I'll meet you." He leaned over the fence to give her another kiss. "Thanks for the tansy."

"My pleasure. Welcome home. Nice to meet you, Mel."

"Yeah. Nice to meet you." Mel pushed her hair out of her eyes and watched Anastasia cross the lawn.

"Yes, she is lovely, isn't she?" Sebastian said lightly. "And as lovely inside as out."

"You seemed pretty close, for cousins."

His lips curved. "Yes, we are. Ana, Morgana and I spent a great deal of our childhood together, here and in Ireland. And, of course, when you have something in common, something that separates you from what's termed the norm, you tend to stick together."

Lifting a brow, Mel turned back to him. "You want me to believe she's psychic, too?"

"Not precisely. Ana has a different talent." He reached out to brush at Mel's bangs himself. "But you didn't come here to talk about my family."

"No." She shifted slightly, just out of reach, and tried to decide on the least humiliating way to thank him. "I checked out the plate. I already had half of it myself when I got the message."

"Oh?"

"I turned up a witness." No way was she going to admit how hard she'd worked to come up with those three little letters. "So anyway, I called my contact at the DMV, had it checked out."

"And?"

"And the car's registered to a James T. Parkland.

The address is in Jamesburg." Propping one booted foot on a low rail, she leaned on the fence while the breeze ruffled her hair. She liked the smell of horses. Just watching them relaxed her. "I took a ride down there. He'd skipped. Landlady was pretty talkative, since he'd ducked two months' rent."

The mare walked over to the fence and bumped Mel's shoulder. Automatically she lifted a hand to stroke down the smooth white cheek. "I got an earful on Jimmy. He was the kind of guy who just invited trouble. Not a bad-looking boy—and I quote—but always had his pockets turned out. Always seemed to scrape up enough for a six-pack, though. The landlady claims to have taken a…motherly interest in him…but I have a hunch it wasn't quite so platonic. Otherwise she wouldn't be so steamed."

"Two months' rent," Sebastian reminded her, watching the way Mel's hand rubbed over the horse.

"Uh-uh. This was personal. She had that bitter tone a woman gets when she's been dumped."

Sebastian tilted his head, trusting Mel's intuition. "Which made her more talkative—to a sympathetic ear."

"You bet. She said he liked to gamble. Mostly on sports, but any game would do. He'd gotten in pretty

deep over the last few months, started having
visitors." She flicked Sebastian a glance. "The kind
who have broken noses and lumps under their suit
coats where their guns ruin the line. He tried to hit
her up for some quick cash, but she claimed she was
tapped out. Then he said how he had a line on how
to get himself out of it, once and for all. Last few
days he was there, he was real nervous, jumpy,
hyped up. Then he split. The last time she saw him
was a week before David's kidnapping."

"An interesting story."

"It gives me something to work with. I figured
you'd want to know."

"What's the next step?"

"Well, it hurts, but I turned over what I had to the
local cops. The more people we have looking for old
Jimmy, the better."

Sebastian ran a hand over Psyche's flank. "He's
about as far away from Monterey as you can get and
still stay in the country."

"Yeah, I figure he's—"

"I don't figure." Sebastian turned those compelling
eyes of his on her. "I know. He's traveling in New
England, too nervous to settle yet."

"Look, Donovan…"

"When you searched his room, did you notice

that the second drawer down on his dresser had a loose pull?"

She had, but she said nothing.

"I'm not playing parlor games with you, Mel," Sebastian said impatiently. "I want to get that boy back, and quickly. Rose is losing hope. Once she loses it completely, she may very well do something drastic."

Instant fear. It gripped Mel by the throat with vicious fingers. "What do you mean?"

"You know what I mean. Use what influence you have. See that the Vermont and New Hampshire police look for him. He's driving a Toyota now. Red. The plates are the same."

She wanted to dismiss it, but she couldn't. "I'm going to go see Rose."

Before she could back away from the fence, Sebastian laid a hand over hers. "I called Rose a couple of hours ago. She'll be all right for a while longer."

"I told you I didn't want you to feed her any of this business."

"You work your way, I'll work mine." His hand tightened on Mel's. "She needed something, a little something to hold on to, to get her through another night when she goes in and looks at an empty crib. I gave it to her."

She felt something from him, something so akin to her own fear and frustration that she relented. "All right, maybe it was the thing to do. I can't second-guess you there. But if you're right about Parkland being in New England…"

"You won't get first shot at him." Sebastian smiled, relaxed now. "And that just burns the hell right out of you."

"You hit that one dead on." She hesitated, then let out a long breath and decided to tell it all. "I got hold of an associate in Georgia."

"You have far-reaching connections, Sutherland."

"I spent about twenty years knocking around the country. Anyway, there's a lawyer there, and he put me on to an investigator he trusts. As a professional courtesy, he's going to do some checking."

"Does that mean you're accepting the fact that David's in Georgia?"

"It means I'm not taking any chances. If I was sure, I'd go myself."

"When you are, and when you do, I'll go with you."

"Right." And there would be reports of frost in hell. There was nothing else she could do tonight, Mel thought. But she had a good beginning. Which was more, she was forced to admit, than she'd had before Sebastian had come along. "Is this head business of yours, this ESP, like what they study at Columbia, places like that?"

He had to smile. It was simply her nature to try to logic out the intangible. "No. Not quite. What you're referring to is that added sense most people have— to some extent—and usually chose to ignore. Those little flashes of insight, premonition, déjà vu. What I am is both less and more."

She wanted something more tangible, more logical, but she doubted she'd get it. "Seems pretty weird to me."

"People are often frightened by what they consider weird. There have been times throughout history when people have been frightened enough to hang or burn or drown those who seemed different." He studied her carefully, his hand still over hers on the rail. "But you aren't frightened, are you?"

"Of you?" Her laugh was quick. "No, I'm not scared of you, Donovan."

"You may be before it's done," he said, half to himself. "But I often feel it's best to live in the present, no matter what you know about tomorrow."

Mel flexed her fingers, nearly gasping at a sudden flash of heat that seemed to jump from his palm into her hand. His face remained calm.

"You like horses."

"What?" Uneasy, she pulled her hand free. "Yeah, sure. What's not to like?"

"Do you ride?"

She moved her shoulders. The heat was gone, but her hand felt as though she'd held it too close to a candle flame. "I've been on one before. Not in the last few years, though."

Sebastian said nothing, but the stallion's head came up, as if he'd heard a signal. He trotted over to the fence, pawing the ground.

"This one looks like he's got a temper." But, even as she said it, Mel was laughing and reaching out to touch. "You know you're beautiful, don't you?"

"He can be a handful," Sebastian commented. "But he can also be gentle if he chooses. Psyche'll be foaling in a few weeks, so she can't be ridden. But if you'd like, you can take a turn on Eros."

"Sometime, maybe." She dropped her hand before the temptation to take him up on it here and now proved too much to resist. "I'd better get going."

He nodded before the temptation to ask her to stay, to stay with him, proved too much to resist. "Tracking down Parkland that quickly was good work."

She was surprised enough to flush a little at the compliment. "It was routine. If I can trace the route to David, that'll be good work."

"We'll start in the desert." And soon, he thought. Very soon. "Sutherland, how about the movies?"

She blinked. "Excuse me?"

"I said how about the movies." He shifted his body toward hers, only the slightest bit. Mel couldn't have said why the movement seemed so much like a threat. Or why the threat seemed so exciting. "Tomorrow night," he continued. "My cousins and I are going. I think you might find my family interesting."

"I'm not much on socializing."

"This would be worth your while." He vaulted the fence as gracefully as Ana had, but this time Mel didn't think of a deer. She thought of a wolf. Now, without the fence between them, the threat, and the excitement, ripened. "A couple of hours of entertainment—to clear your mind. Afterward, I think you and I might have somewhere to go."

"If you're going to talk in riddles, we won't get anywhere."

"Trust me on this." He cupped a hand on her cheek. His fingers lay there as lightly as butterfly wings, but she found it impossible to brush them away. "An evening with the Donovans will be good for both of us."

She knew her voice would be breathless before she spoke, and she damned him for it. He only had his hand on her face. "I've pretty well decided nothing about you could be good for me."

He smiled then, thinking how flattering the evening light was to her skin, how caution added an odd attraction to her eyes. "It's a invitation to the movies, Mel, not a proposition. At least not precisely like the one you dodged this morning from the lonely man on the third floor of Rose's building."

Wary, she stepped back. It could have been a good guess. A remarkably good one. "How did you know about that?"

"I'll pick you up in time for the nine-o'clock show. Maybe I'll explain it to you." He held up a hand before she could refuse. "You said you weren't afraid of me, Sutherland. Prove it."

It was a perfect ploy. She understood that they both knew it. "I pay my own way. This isn't a date."

"No, indeed."

"Okay, then. Tomorrow night." She took a backward step, then turned. It was easier to think, she realized, when she wasn't facing him, or staring into those patient, amused eyes. "See you."

"Yes," he murmured. "You certainly will."

As he watched her walk away, his smile slowly faded. No, it wasn't a date. He doubted there would be anything as simple as a date in their relationship.

And, though he was far from comfortable with the idea, he already knew they would have a relationship.

When he'd had his hand over Mel's, just before she yanked it away from that sudden flare of heat, he'd seen. He hadn't looked, not voluntarily, but he'd seen.

The two of them in the last rosy light of dusk. Her skin like ripe peaches under his hands. Fear in her eyes, fear and something stronger than fear. Through the open windows the first stirrings of the night creatures, those secret songs of the dark.

And he'd seen where they had been. Where they would be, however each of them tried to refuse it.

Frowning, Sebastian turned his head and looked up to the wide window glinting now in the lowering sunlight. Beyond the window was the bed where he slept, where he dreamed. The bed he would share with Mel before the summer was over.

## Chapter 5

Mel had plenty to keep her occupied throughout the day. There was the mopping up of a missing-persons case, the groundwork for a possible insurance fraud for Underwriter's, and the little boy who had stopped by to hire her to find his lost dog.

She'd agreed to take the case of the missing pooch, for a retainer of two dollars and seven cents—mostly pennies. It did her heart good to see the boy go off, assured the matter was in professional hands.

She ate what passed for dinner at her desk. Munching on potato chips and a fat dill pickle, she made follow-up calls to the local police, and to the authorities in Vermont and New Hampshire. She touched base with her counterpart in Georgia, and hung up dissatisfied.

Everybody was looking for James T. Parkland. Everybody was looking for David Merrick. And nobody was finding them.

After a check of her watch, she called the local pound with a description of the missing mutt and her young client's name and phone number. Too restless to stay inside, she took the Polaroid snapshot the boy had given her of his canine best friend and made the rounds.

Three hours later, she located Kong, an aptly named mixed breed of astonishing proportions, snoozing in the storeroom of a shop on Fisherman's Wharf.

Using a length of twine donated by the shop-keeper, Mel managed to lead Kong to her car and stuff him into the passenger seat. Worried that the dog might leap out during the drive back to her office, Mel strapped him in with the seat belt and had her face bathed with a big wet tongue.

"Lot of nerve you've got," she muttered as she climbed in beside him. "Don't you think I figured out you went AWOL to cruise chicks? That kid of yours is worried sick about you, and where do I find you? Cozied up in a shell shop with pastrami on your breath."

Rather than appearing chastised, the dog seemed to grin, his tongue lolling out of the corner of his mouth, his head lifted to the wind, as Mel maneuvered through the parking lot.

"Don't you know the meaning of loyalty?" she asked him. Kong shifted his bulky body, laid his massive head on her shoulder and moaned. "Sure, sure. I know your kind, buster. Love the one you're with. Well, you can forget about me. I'm on to you."

But she lifted a hand from the gearshift to scratch his ears.

Sebastian was just parking his motorcycle when Mel pulled up in front of her office. He took one look at her and at the hundred and fifty pounds of muscle and fur riding beside her in the tiny car and grinned.

"Just like a woman. Here I think we're going out and you've picked yourself up another date."

"He's more my type." She finger-combed her hair away from her face, used her arm to wipe the dog kisses off her cheek, then located the end of the twine. "What are you doing here, anyway? Oh," she said before he could answer. "Movies. Right. I forgot."

"You sure know how to flatter a man, Sutherland." He moved out of her way when she unbuckled the dog's seat belt. "Nice dog."

"I guess. Come on, Kong, ride's over." She tugged and pulled, but the dog merely sat there, panting and grinning—and, she noted, shedding dusty yellow hairs on her seat.

Enjoying the performance, Sebastian leaned on the hood of her car. "Ever consider obedience school?"

"Reform school," she muttered. "But he's not mine." Mel gritted her teeth and put her back into it. "Belongs to a client. Damn it, Kong, get your butt out."

As if he'd merely been waiting for her to ask, the dog responded by jumping out, ramming Mel back into Sebastian. He caught her neatly around the waist as she lost her footing. While she worked on getting her breath back, Mel scowled at the dog, who now sat placidly on the sidewalk.

"You're a real jerk, you know that?" she said to Kong. As if he agreed wholeheartedly, the dog went through his repertoire of tricks. Lying down, rolling over, then sitting up again with one paw lifted to shake.

She laughed before she realized her back was still nestled against Sebastian's chest. His very hard chest. Automatically she brought her hands down to his and pried them off.

"Let go."

Sebastian ran his hands up her arms once before

she managed to break away. "You sure are touchy, Sutherland."

She tossed her head. "Depends on who's doing the touching." Wanting to wait until her heartbeat leveled, she swiped halfheartedly at the dog hairs clinging to her jeans. "Look, do me a favor and stay out here with fur-face while I make a call. There's a kid who, for reasons that escape me, actually wants this mutt back."

"Go ahead." Sebastian crouched down and ran his elegant hands over the dusty fur.

Only minutes after Mel came back out, a young boy rushed down the sidewalk, a red leash trailing behind him.

"Oh, wow. Kong. Oh, wow."

In response, the dog leapt to his feet, barking happily. He rushed the boy—like a fullback blocking a tight end. They went down on the sidewalk in a delighted, rolling heap.

With one arm hooked over Kong's massive neck, the boy grinned up at Mel. "Gee, lady, you sure are a real detective and all. Just like on TV. Thanks. Thanks a lot. You did real good."

"Thanks." Mel held out a hand to accept the boy's formal handshake.

"Do I owe you any more?"

"No, we're square. You ought to get him one of those tags with his name and your phone number on it. In case he decides to hit the road again."

"Okay. Yeah, okay." He hooked the red leash onto Kong's collar. "Wait till Mom sees. Come on, Kong, let's go home." They went off at a dash, the dog pulling the boy behind him. "Thanks," he called out again, and his laughter echoed on the evening air.

"He's right," Sebastian murmured, not bothering to resist the urge to run his fingers through her hair. "You did good."

She shrugged, wishing she weren't so moved by the tone of his voice, by the touch of his hand. "I earn my keep."

"I bet you made a bundle on that one."

Laughing a little, she turned her head. "Hey, I made two dollars and seven cents. That ought to buy me some popcorn at the flicks."

He cut off her laughter by touching his lips to hers. It wasn't a kiss…really…she thought. It was… friendlier.

"What did you do that for?"

"Just one of those things." Sebastian straddled his bike, then tossed her a helmet. "Climb on, Sutherland. I hate to be late for the movies."

* * *

All in all, it wasn't a bad way to unwind. Mel had always enjoyed the movies. They had been one of her favorite recreations as a child. It didn't matter if you were the new kid in school once the lights went out and the screen flickered into life.

Movie theaters were comfortingly familiar anywhere in the country. The smell of popcorn and candy, the sticky floors, the shufflings people made as they settled down to watch. Whatever movie was playing in El Paso was probably entertaining patrons in Tallahassee, too.

Mel had been drawn back to them time and time again during her mother's wanderings, stealing a couple of hours a week where it didn't matter where she was. Or who she was.

She felt the same sense of anonymity here, with the moody music and shadowy suspense on the screen. A killer was stalking the streets, and Mel— along with the other viewers—was content to sit back and watch the ancient duel of good against evil.

She sat between Sebastian and his cousin, Morgana. His gorgeous cousin Morgana, Mel had noted.

She'd heard the rumors about Morgana Donovan Kirkland. The rumors that whispered she was a witch. Mel had found them laughable—and only found them more so now. Morgana was anything but a cackling crone ready to jump on board a broomstick.

Still, she imagined the rumors added to the business Morgana pulled in at her shop.

On the other side of Morgana was her husband, Nash. Mel knew he was a successful and highly respected screenwriter, one who specialized in horror scripts. His work had certainly scared a few muffled screams from Mel—and made her laugh at herself.

Nash Kirkland didn't seem the Hollywood type to her. He struck her as open and easygoing—and very much in love with his wife.

They held hands during the movies. But not with the sloppy sort of mush that would have made Mel uncomfortable. Instead, there was a quiet, steady bond of affection in the gesture that she envied.

On the other side of Sebastian was Anastasia. Mel wondered why a woman as hauntingly lovely as Ana didn't have a date. Then she reminded herself that such a thought was sexist and stupid. Not every woman—herself included—found it necessary to go everywhere hanging on to the arm of a man.

Mel dug into her popcorn and settled into the movie.

"You going to eat all that?"

"Hmm?" Distracted, she turned her head. Then jerked it back quickly. She'd practically been lip-to-lip with Sebastian. "What?"

"You going to share, or what?"

She stared a moment. Wasn't it odd how his eyes seemed to glow in the dark? When he tapped a finger on the box of popcorn in her lap, she blinked.

"Oh, yeah. Help yourself."

He did, enjoying her reaction to him every bit as much as the buttery popcorn.

She smelled…fresh. Sebastian kept part of his mind on the twists and turns of the plot and let the rest wander at will. He found it pleasant to be able to scent her soap-and-water skin over the aromas of the theater. If he let himself, he could hear her pulse beating. Steady, very steady, and strong—and then a quick jerk and flutter when the action heated up on-screen.

What would her pulse do if he touched her now? If he were to shift his body and take that wide, un-painted mouth with his own?

He thought he knew. He thought he could wait and see.

But he couldn't quite resist a gentle poke into her own thoughts.

*Idiot! If she knows somebody's after her, why is she*

*bopping down the street in the dark? How come they
always have to make women either dumb or helpless?
There she goes—running into the park. Oh, sure, it
makes perfect sense to haul her butt into the bushes
where he can slit her throat. Ten to one she trips...
Yep.*

*Oh, well, that one deserves to get iced.*

She crunched on more popcorn, and Sebastian
heard her wish absently that she'd added more salt.

Her thoughts stuttered to a halt, then tangled into
confusion. What he was reading in her head he could
see on her face.

She sensed him. She didn't understand what it
was, but she sensed an intrusion and was instinctively blocking it.

The fact that she did, the fact that she could, intrigued him. It was very rare for anyone outside his
family to feel his scannings.

There was some power here, he mused. Untapped,
and certainly denied. He toyed with the idea of
pushing a little deeper. Beside him, Ana stirred.

"Don't be rude, Sebastian," she said gently.

Relenting, reluctantly, he gave himself over to the
movie.

He reached for some popcorn, and his fingers
brushed Mel's. She flinched. He grinned.

\* \* \*

"Pizza," Morgana said when they stepped outside. "With the works."

Nash ran a hand down her hair. "I thought you said you wanted Mexican."

She smiled, patting her belly. "We changed our minds."

"Pizza," Ana agreed. "No anchovies." She smiled at Mel. "How about it?"

Mel felt herself linked in this ring of good fellowship. "Sure. That sounds—"

"We can't," Sebastian interrupted, laying a hand on her shoulder.

Curious, Morgana pursed her lips. "I've never known you to turn down food, darling." She shot a quick, humorous look at Mel. "Cousin Sebastian has outrageous appetites. You'd be amazed."

"Mel's much too practical-minded to be amazed," Sebastian said coolly. "What astonishes, she merely dismisses."

"He's only baiting you." Ana gave Sebastian a quick dig in the ribs. "We've seen so little of you lately. Can't you spare another hour, Sebastian?"

"Not tonight."

"Well, I can…" Mel began.

"I'll see the lady home." Nash winked at Mel. "I

don't have any problem taking on three beautiful women alone."

"You're such a generous man, darling." Morgana patted her husband's cheek. "But I think Sebastian has other plans for his lady."

"I'm not his—"

"Exactly." He tightened his grip on Mel's shoulder. "We'll do it next time." He kissed both of his cousins. "Blessed be." And he propelled Mel down the sidewalk toward his bike.

"Listen, Donovan, we said this wasn't a date, and maybe I'd have liked to go along with them. I'm hungry."

He unsnapped a helmet, then dropped it on her head. "I'll feed you eventually."

"I'm not a horse," Mel muttered, fastening the helmet. "I can feed myself." Pouting only a little, she glanced over her shoulder at the retreating trio as she climbed behind Sebastian onto the bike. It wasn't all that often that she went out with a group—and particularly a group she felt so comfortable with. But if she was annoyed with Sebastian for breaking it up early, she had to be grateful to him for including her in the first place.

"Don't sulk."

"I never sulk." She rested her hands lightly on his hips for balance as he drove away from the curb.

She enjoyed the feeling of the bike—the freedom of it, and the risk. Perhaps, when her cash flow was a little more fluid, she'd look into getting one for herself. Of course, it would be more practical to have her car painted and tuned first. Also, there was that leak in the bathroom that needed to be dealt with. And she really wanted some new surveillance equipment. The high-tech stuff cost the earth.

But she might be able to swing it in another year or so. The way things were going, her books ended nearly every month in the black. Breaking up that burglary ring and saving Underwriter's a hefty chunk in claims might just shake a bonus loose.

She let her mind drift in that direction, her body automatically leaning with Sebastian's in the curves. Mel wasn't aware that her hands had slid more truly around his waist, but Sebastian was.

She liked the sensation of the wind in her face, on her skin. And, though she wasn't proud of it, she enjoyed the way her body fit snug to his with the bike vibrating seductively beneath them.

He had a very…interesting body. It was difficult not to notice, Mel thought, since they were sharing such a small space. His back was muscled beneath the butter-smooth leather jacket. His shoulders were quite wide—or maybe they only seemed so because his hips were lean and narrow.

There were muscles in his arms, as well. Not that she was overly impressed with that sort of thing, she reminded herself. It was just that it surprised her that someone in his line of work—so to speak—was so well built.

More like a tennis player than an oracle.

Then again, she supposed he had plenty of time for working out, or riding his horses, or whatever form of exercise he preferred, between visions.

She began to wonder what it might be like to own her own horse.

It wasn't until she realized he was swinging onto the eastbound ramp of 156 that she came to attention.

"Hey!" She rapped her fingers on his helmet. "Hey, Daniel Boone, the trail's back that way."

He heard her clearly enough, but shook his head. "What? Did you say something?"

"Yeah, I said something." But she did precisely as he'd hoped she would. She wiggled closer on the seat and leaned against him. He felt every curve. "I said you're going the wrong way. My place is back there, about ten miles back there."

"I know where you live."

She huffed and kept her voice lifted over the purr of the engine. "Then what are we doing out here?"

"Nice night for a drive."

Yeah, maybe it was, but nobody had asked her. "I don't want to go for a drive."

"You'll want to go on this one."

"Oh, yeah? Well, where are we going?"

Sebastian zipped around a sedan and punched it up to sixty. "Utah."

It was a good ten miles before Mel managed to close her mouth.

Three o'clock in the morning, in the ghastly light of the parking lot of a combination convenience store and gas station. Mel's bottom felt as though it had been shot full of novocaine.

But her mind wasn't numb. She might have been tired, cranky and sore after riding on the back of a bike for four hours, but her mind was functioning just fine.

Right now she was using it to develop ways of murdering Sebastian Donovan and making it the perfect crime.

It was a damn shame she hadn't brought her gun. Then she could just shoot him. Clean and quick. On some of the roads they'd been traveling, she could dump the body into a gully where it might not be found for weeks. Possibly years.

Still, it would be more satisfying to beat him to death. He had her by a few inches, and maybe fifty pounds, but she thought she could take him.

Then she could ditch the bike, hop a bus and be back in her office bright and early the next morning.

Mel stretched her legs by pacing the parking lot. Occasionally a semi rattled by, using the back roads to avoid weighing stations. Apart from that, it was dark and quiet. Once she heard something that sounded suspiciously like a coyote, but she dismissed it.

Even out here in the boonies, she assured herself, people had dogs.

Oh, he'd been clever, she thought now, kicking an empty soda can out of her way. He hadn't stopped the bike until they'd been past Fresno. Not exactly walking distance back to Monterey.

And when she'd hopped off, punched him and let loose with a string of curses that should have turned his ears blue, he'd simply waited her out. Waited her out, and then gone on to explain that he'd wanted to follow James T. Parkland's trail.

He'd needed to see the motel where David had stayed with the first woman he'd been passed to.

As if there were a motel. Mel kicked the hapless can again. Did he really expect her to believe they would drive up to some dumb motel with a dinosaur out front?

Right.

So, here she was, tired, hungry and numb from the waist down, stuck on some back road with a crazy psychic. She was two hundred and fifty miles from home, and she had eleven dollars and eighty-six cents on her person.

"Sutherland."

Mel whirled and caught the candy bar he tossed her. She would have cursed him then, but she had to snag the soft drink can that came looping after it.

"Look, Donovan…" Since he was busy with the gas pump, she stalked over, ripping the wrapper off the candy bar as she went. "I've got a business to run. I have clients. I can't be running around half the night with you chasing wild geese."

"You ever done any camping?"

"What? No."

"I've done some up in the Sierra Nevadas. Not far from here. Very peaceful."

"If you don't turn this bike around and take me back, you're going to have an eternity of peace. Starting now."

When he looked at her, really looked, she saw that he didn't appear tired at all. Oh, no. Rather than suffering from four hours of traveling, he looked as if he'd just spent a week at some exclusive spa.

Under the relaxation, the calm, was a drumming excitement that took hold of her pulse and set it hopping. Resenting every minute of it, Mel took a healthy bite of chocolate.

"You're crazy. Certifiable. We can't go to Utah. Do you know how far it is to Utah?"

He realized the temperature had dropped considerably. Sebastian peeled off his jacket and handed it to her. "To the place we want, from Monterey? About five hundred miles." He clicked off the pump, replaced the nozzle. "Cheer up, Sutherland, we're more than halfway there."

She gave up. "There must be a bus depot around here," she muttered, tugging on his jacket as she headed toward the harshly lit store.

"This is where he stopped off with David." Sebastian spoke quietly, and she stopped in her tracks. "Where they made the first switch. He didn't make the kind of time we did, what with traffic, nerves, and watching the rearview mirror for cops. The meet was set for eight."

"This is bull," Mel said, but her throat was tight.

"The night man recognized him from the sketch. He noticed him because Jimmy parked all the way across the lot, even though there were spaces just out front. And he was nervous, so the night man kept an eye on him, thinking he might try to shoplift. But Jimmy paid."

Mel watched Sebastian carefully as he spoke. When he was finished, she held out a hand. "Give me the sketch."

With his eyes on hers, Sebastian reached in the top pocket of the jacket. Through the lining, his hand brushed lightly over her breast, lingering for a heartbeat before he lifted the folded sketch out.

She knew she was breathing too fast. She knew she was feeling more than that brief, meaningless contact warranted. To compensate, she snatched the paper out of his hand and strode toward the store.

As she went inside to verify what he had just told her, Sebastian secured his gas cap and rolled the bike away from the pumps.

It took her less than five minutes. She was pale when she returned, her eyes burning dark in her face. But her hand was steady when she tucked the sketch away again. She didn't want to think, not yet. Sometimes it was better to act.

"All right," she told him. "Let's go."

She didn't doze. That could be suicide on a bike. But she did find her mind wandering, with old images passing over new. It was all so familiar, this middle-

of-the-night traveling. Never being quite sure where
you were going or what you would do when you got
there.

Her mother had always been so happy driving down
nameless roads with the radio blaring. Mel could
remember the comfort of stretching out on the front
seat, her head in her mother's lap, and the simplicity
of trusting that somehow they would find a home again.

Heavy with fatigue, her head dropped to Sebastian's back. She jerked up, forcing her eyes wide.

"Want to stop for a while?" he called to her.
"Take a break?"

"No. Keep going."

Toward dawn he did stop, refueling himself with
coffee. Mel opted for a caffeine-laden soft drink and
wolfed down a sugar-spiked pastry.

"I feel I owe you a decent meal," Sebastian commented while they took a five-minute breather somewhere near Devil's Playground.

"This *is* my idea of a decent meal." Content, she
licked sugar and frosting off her fingers. "You can
keep the pheasant under glass."

Her eyes were shadowed. He was sorry for that,
but he'd acted on instinct—an instinct he'd known
was right. When he slipped an arm around her, she
stiffened, but only for a moment. Perhaps she recog-

nized that the gesture was one of friendly support and nothing more.

"We'll be there soon," he told her. "Another hour."

She nodded. She had no choice but to trust him now. To trust him, and the feeling inside her. What Mel would have called a gut hunch. "I just want to know it's worth it. That it's going to make a difference."

"We'll have that answer, too."

"I hope so. I hope the answer's yes." She turned her face into him, her lips brushing over his throat. There was a flare of warmth, of flavor, before her gritty eyes widened. "I'm sorry. I'm punchy." She would have moved away, far away, but his arm merely tightened around her.

"Relax, Mel. Look. Sun's coming up."

They watched the dawn bloom together, his arm around her and her head resting lightly against his shoulder. Over the desert, the colors rose up from the horizon, bleeding into the sky and tinting the low-hanging clouds. Dull sand blushed pink, then deepened to rose before it slowly became gilded. In another hour, the baking sun would leech the color out of the landscape. But for now, for just this single hushed moment, it was as lovely as any painting.

She felt something here, watching this ageless transition with his arm around her. A communion.

The first gentle fingers of a bond that needed no words for understanding.

This time, when he kissed her, his mouth soft and seeking, she didn't resist and she didn't question. The moment itself justified it. She was too tired to fight whatever was growing inside her. She was too dazed by the magic of dawn over the desert to refuse what he asked of her.

He wanted to ask for more—knew that at this moment, in this place, he could ask. But he could sense her fatigue, her confusion, and her nagging fears for a friend's child. So he kept the kiss easy, a comfort to both of them. When he released her, he understood that what they had begun would not be broken.

Without a word, they mounted the bike again and headed east, toward the sun.

In southern Utah, not far from the Arizona border—and near enough to Vegas for an easy trip to lose a paycheck—was a hot little huddle of storefronts. The town, such as it was, had a gas station, a tiny café that offered corn tortillas, and a twenty-five unit motel with a plaster brontosaurus in the center of the gravel lot.

"Oh," Mel whispered as she stared at the sadly

chipped dinosaur. "Oh, sweet Lord." As she eased off the bike, her legs were trembling from more than travel fatigue.

"Let's go see if anyone's awake." Sebastian took her arm to pull her toward the check-in desk.

"You did see it, didn't you?"

"It seems that way, doesn't it?" When she swayed, he wrapped a supporting arm around her waist. Odd that she would suddenly seem so fragile. "We'll get you a bed while we're at it."

"I'm all right." She'd go into shock later, Mel promised herself. Right now she needed to keep moving. Together they walked through the door and into the fan-cooled lobby.

Sebastian rang the bell on the desk. Moments later, they heard the shuffle of slippered feet behind a faded flowered curtain.

A man in a white athletic shirt and baggy jeans wandered out, his eyes puffy with sleep, his face unshaven.

"Help you?"

"Yes." Sebastian reached for his wallet. "We need a room. Unit 15." He laid down crisp green cash.

"Happens it's empty." The clerk reached for a key from the pegboard behind him. "Twenty-eight a night. Café down the road there serves breakfast twenty-four hours. You want to sign here?"

After he had, Sebastian laid another twenty on the counter, with David's picture on top of it. "Have you seen this boy? It would have been three months ago."

The clerk looked longingly at the twenty. David's picture might have been a sheet of glass. "Can't remember everybody who comes through."

"He was with a woman. Attractive, early thirties. A redhead, driving a midsize Chevy."

"Maybe they was through. I mind my business and nobody else's."

Mel nudged Sebastian aside. "You look like a pretty sharp guy to me. I'd think if a good-looking lady like that came through here, with a cute little baby, you'd notice. Maybe you'd tell her where she could buy spare diapers, or get fresh milk."

He shrugged his shoulders and scratched. "I don't look into anybody else's trouble."

"You'll look to your own, though." Mel's voice had toughened, enough for the clerk to look up warily. "Now, when Agent Donovan— I mean Mr. Donovan." The clerk's eyes widened. "When he asked you if you'd seen that little boy, I think you were going to think it over. Weren't you?"

The clerk licked his lips. "You cops? FBI or something?"

Mel only smiled. "We'll say 'or something' and keep everything mellow."

"I run a quiet place here."

"I can see that. That's why I know if that woman stopped off here with the kid, you'd remember. I don't guess you get all that much traffic."

"Look, she only spent one night. She paid cash in advance, kept the kid pretty quiet through the night and went on her way first thing in the morning."

Mel fought back the ragged edge of hope and kept her voice cool. "Give me a name, pal."

"Hell's bells, how'm I supposed to remember names?"

"You keep records." Mel put a fingertip on the twenty and inched it across the counter. "Records of registered guests, and any phone calls they might make from their rooms. Why don't you dig it up for us? My partner might even give you a bonus."

Muttering oaths, the clerk pulled a cardboard box from behind the desk. "Got phone records here. You can look through the register yourself."

Mel reached for the registration book, then put her hands behind her back and let Sebastian do it. She was ready to admit he'd find what they were looking for quicker than she would.

Sebastian homed in on the name. "Susan White? I don't suppose she showed you any ID?"

"Paid cash," the clerk mumbled. "Jeezie peezie, you expect me to frisk her or something? One long-distance call," he announced. "Went through the operator."

Mel dug in her purse for her notepad. "Date and time." She scribbled them down. "Now listen, friend, and this is the bonus question—no jive. Would you state under oath that this child…and look carefully—" she held up David's picture "—this child was brought into this motel last May?"

The clerk shifted uncomfortably. "If I had to, I would. I don't want to go to court or nothing, but she brought him. I remember he had that dimple there and that funny reddish hair."

"Good job." She wasn't going to cry—oh, no, she wasn't. But she walked outside while Sebastian replaced the photo and passed the clerk another twenty.

"Okay?" he asked when he joined her.

"Sure. Fine."

"I need to see the room, Mel."

"Right."

"You can wait out here if you want."

"No. Let's go."

She didn't speak again, not when they walked down the broken sidewalk, not when he unlocked the door and stepped inside its stuffy walls. She sat on the bed, clearing her mind while Sebastian used his for what he did best.

He could see the baby, sleeping on a pallet on the floor, whimpering a bit in his confusing dreams.

She'd left the light on in the bathroom so that she could see easily if the child woke and began to cry. She'd watched a little television, made her call.

But her name wasn't Susan White. She'd used so many over the years that it was difficult for Sebastian to pick up on the true one. He thought it was Linda, but it wasn't Linda now, and it wasn't Susan, either.

And it hadn't been more than a few weeks before that when she had transported still another baby.

He would have to tell Mel about that once she'd rested.

When he sat on the bed beside her, put a hand on her shoulder, she continued to stare straight ahead.

"I don't want to know right now how you did it. I might sometime, but not now. Okay?"

"Okay."

"She had him here in this room."

"Yes."

"And he isn't hurt?"

"No."

Mel wet her lips. "Where did she take him?"

"Texas, but she doesn't know where he was taken from there. She's only one leg of the trip."

Mel took two deep, careful breaths. "Georgia. Are you sure it's Georgia?"

"Yes."

Her hands fisted on her lap. "Where? Do you know where?"

He was tired, more tired than he wanted to admit. And it would drain him even more to look now. But she needed him to. Not in here, he thought. There was too much interference in here, too many sad stories in this sad little room.

"I have to go outside. Leave me alone for a minute."

She just nodded, and he left her. Time passed, and she was relieved to find that the need to cry went with it.

Mel didn't see tears as weak, particularly. She saw them as useless.

So her eyes were dry when Sebastian came back into the room.

She thought he looked pale, and suddenly tired. Odd that she hadn't noticed the fatigue around his eyes a few moments ago. Then again, she reminded herself, she hadn't been looking at him very carefully.

She did so now, and because she did she felt compelled to rise and go to him. Perhaps the lack of roots and family had made her a person wary of outward displays of affection. She'd never been a toucher, but she reached out now, taking both his hands in hers.

"You look like you need the bed more than I do. Why don't you sack out for an hour? Then we'll figure out what to do next."

He didn't answer, only turned her hands over and stared at her palms. Would she believe how many things he could see there?

"Tough shells aren't necessarily thick ones," he said quietly, lifting his gaze to hers. "You've got a soft center, Mel. It's very attractive."

Then he did something that left her both shaken and speechless. He lifted her hands to his lips. No one had ever done that before, and she discovered that what she'd assumed was a silly affectation was both moving and seductive.

"He's in a place called Forest Park, a suburb a little south of Atlanta."

Her fingers tightened on his, then relaxed. If she

had never taken anything in her life on faith before, she would take this.

"Stretch out on the bed." Her voice was brisk, her hands firm, as she nudged him over to it. "I'm going to call the FBI and the nearest airport."

# Chapter 6

She slept like a stone. Sebastian sipped a little more wine, kicked back in his chair and watched Mel. She was stretched out on the sofa across from him in the main cabin of his private plane. She hadn't argued when he'd suggested having his pilot fly to Utah to pick them up for the trip east. She'd simply nodded distractedly and continued to scribble notes in her ever-present pad.

The moment they'd hit cruising height, she'd ranged her long body out on the couch, closed her eyes and gone under, as quickly and easily as an exhausted infant. He understood that energy, like any power, had to be recharged, and he'd left her alone.

Sebastian had indulged in a long shower and changed into some of the spare clothes he kept aboard the Lear. While he enjoyed a light lunch, he made a few phone calls. And waited.

It was an odd journey, to say the least. Himself and the sleeping woman, hurtling away from the sun after a night of racing toward it. When it was over, there would be broken hearts and mended ones. Fate always charged a fee.

And he would have crossed a continent with a woman he found annoying, desirable, and incomprehensible.

She stirred, murmured something, then opened her eyes. He watched the cloudy green sharpen and focus as she pushed past the disorientation. She stretched once—it was a brisk, businesslike movement, and it was incredibly sexy—then rolled herself to a sitting position.

"How much longer?" Her voice was still husky with sleep, but he could see the energy pouring back.

"Less than an hour."

"Good." After running a hand through her hair, she lifted her head, scenting the air. "Do I smell food?"

He had to smile. "In the galley. There's a shower to starboard if you want to wash up."

"Thanks."

She chose the shower first. It wasn't easy, but she didn't want to act unduly impressed that the man could snap his fingers and call up his own plane—a plane fitted out with deep pile carpeting, its own cozy bedroom and a galley that made her kitchen at home look like someone's closet. Obviously the psychic business paid well.

She should have checked his background, Mel thought now as she wrapped herself in a robe and tiptoed into the bedroom. But she'd been so sure that she would be able to talk Rose out of using him that she hadn't bothered. Now here she was, some thirty thousand feet up, with a man she knew much too little about.

She'd remedy that the moment they touched down in Monterey again. Though, of course, if things went as she hoped, there would be no need to. Once David was back where he belonged, her association with Sebastian Donovan would be over.

Still, she might run a background check on him, just out of curiosity.

Lips pursed, Mel poked into his closet. He liked silk and cashmere and linen, she discovered. Spotting a denim shirt, she yanked it out. At least he had something practical, and she sure could use some fresh clothes.

She tugged it on, then whipped around to the doorway. For a moment, she had thought he was there, had been sure of it. Then she realized it was his scent, clinging still to the shirt that was now brushing softly against her skin.

What was that fragrance, exactly? Experimentally she lifted her arm to sniff the sleeve. Nothing she could quite pinpoint. Something wild, erotic. Something you'd expect to catch just a whiff of in the forest in the dark of the moon.

Annoyed with herself, she pulled on her jeans. If this kept up, she'd actually start believing in witches.

After rolling the sleeves of the borrowed shirt up to her elbows, she went to investigate the galley. She helped herself to a banana, ignored a jar of caviar and tossed some ham and cheese on a piece of bread.

"Got any mustard?" she called out, then swallowed a gasp when she felt his body bump against hers. He'd made no more sound than a ghost.

He reached over her head for a jar and handed it to her. "Want some wine?"

"I guess." She slathered mustard on the bread, wishing there was a little more room to maneuver away from him in the small space. "I borrowed a shirt. Okay?"

"Sure." He poured her wine and topped off his own glass. "You rested well."

"Yeah, well, it helps the time pass." The plane danced in some turbulence. His hand came down to steady her and stayed on her arm. "The pilot said there'd be a few bumps." Testing both of them, he rubbed his thumb over the inside of her elbow. The pulse there was fast and steady. "We'll be starting our descent soon."

She lifted her face to his. Studying him, she felt what she had felt in the desert. The beginning of something. Mel wondered if she'd be less restless if she were able to see the end as well.

"Then we'd better sit down. And strap in."

"I'll take your wine."

With a long breath of relief, she picked up her plate and followed him. As she dug happily into the sandwich, she noticed him smiling at her. "Problem?"

"I was just thinking that I really do owe you an actual meal."

"You don't owe me." She took a sip of wine, and then, because it was so different, so delightfully different, from what she was used to, she sipped again. "I like paying my own way."

"I've noticed."

Mel tilted her head. "Some guys are intimidated by that."

"Really?" A smile played around his lips. "I'm not. Still, after we're finished, maybe you'd agree to dinner. A celebration of a job well done."

"Maybe," she said over a mouthful of sandwich. "We can flip to see who buys."

"Lord, you are charming." He chuckled and stretched out his legs, pleased she'd chosen the seat facing him rather than the one beside him. Now he could look his fill when she was awake. "Why private investigations?"

"Hmmm?"

His lips curved again. "It's time I asked, don't you think? What made you choose your profession?"

"I like to figure things out." She moved her shoulders and started to rise to take her empty plate away. But he stood up and took it into the galley himself.

"It's that simple?"

"I believe in the rules." The seats were roomy, so she tucked her legs up and crossed them. She was comfortable, she realized. Refreshed from the nap, and from a surge of hope that had yet to fade. Easy in his company. Well, she supposed, anything was possible.

"And I think when you break the rules somebody should make you pay for it." She felt the subtle shift and change in the cabin as the plane began its descent into Atlanta. "I also like to figure things out—by myself. That's why I only made a pretty good cop but I make a really good PI."

"So, you're not a team player."

"Nope." She cocked her head. "Are you?"

"No." He smiled into his wine. "I suppose not." Then, abruptly, his eyes were intense again, focused on her. Into her, she thought. "But rules often change, Mel. The lines between right and wrong sometimes blur. When that happens, how do you choose?"

"By knowing what things shouldn't change, what lines can't be blurred—or crossed. You just feel it."

"Yeah." With that sudden flash of power banked again, he nodded. "You just feel it."

"It has nothing to do with being psychic." She thought she understood just where he was leading her. She wasn't ready to give him quite that much rope. "I don't go in for visions or second sight or whatever you call it."

He lifted his glass in toast. "But you're here, aren't you?"

Her eyes remained level. If he expected her to squirm, he'd be disappointed. "Yeah, I'm here, Donovan. I'm here because I won't risk not following up any lead—no matter how slim, or how weird."

He continued smiling. "And?"

"And because maybe I'm willing to consider that you might have seen or felt something. Or maybe you just had a good gut hunch. I believe in hunches."

"So do I, Mel." The plane bumped down on the runway. "So do I."

It was always difficult to turn over the reins to another. Mel didn't mind cooperating with local authorities or the FBI, but she preferred doing it on her own terms. For David's sake, she had to bite her tongue a dozen times during the interview with Federal Agent Thomas A. Devereaux.

"I have reports on you, Mr. Donovan. Several, in fact, from associates of mine who consider you not only trustworthy but something of a wonder."

Mel thought Sebastian sat in the small, beige-toned office like a king at his court. He responded to Devereaux's statement with a slight nod.

"I've been involved in a few federal investigations."

"Most recently in Chicago," Devereaux said, flipping through a file. "A bad mess up there. A pity we couldn't stop it sooner."

"Yes." It was all Sebastian would say. Not all of those images had faded.

"And you, Ms. Sutherland." Devereaux rubbed his

round, bald head, then poked a finger at the nosepiece of his glasses. "The local authorities in California seem to find you competent enough."

"I can sleep easy now." She ignored Sebastian's warning glance and leaned forward. "Can we bypass the introductions, Agent Devereaux? I have friends back in California who are desperate. David Merrick's only a few miles away—"

"That's yet to be determined." Devereaux set one file aside and picked up another. "We had all pertinent information faxed in after your call. A federal investigator has already interviewed your witness at the…Dunes Motel in Utah." He pushed his glasses up again. "He positively identified David Merrick's picture. We're working on IDing the woman."

"Then why are we sitting here?"

Devereaux peered over the rims of his glasses, which had already slid down his nose again. "Do you expect us to knock on every door in Forest Park and ask if they've recently stolen a baby?" Anticipating her, he held up a pudgy finger. "We have data coming in right now on male children between the ages of six and nine months. Adoption records, birth certificates. We're looking into who has moved into the area, with a child, within the last three months. I have no doubt that by morning we'll have narrowed it down to a manageable few."

"Morning? Listen, Devereaux, we've just spent the best part of twenty-four hours getting here. Now you're going to tell us to wait until morning?"

Devereaux leveled a look at Mel. "Yes. If you give us the name of your hotel, we'll contact you with any further developments."

Mel popped out of her chair. "I know David. I can identify him. If I did a sweep of the area, set up some surveillance—"

Devereaux cut her off. "This is a federal case. We may very well want you to identify the boy. However, we have copies of his prints to substantiate." While Mel bit her tongue, Devereaux shifted his gaze from her to Sebastian. "I'm moving on this under the advice of Special Agent Tucker in Chicago—who I've known for more than twenty years. Because he puts some stock in this psychic business, and because I have a grandson about David's age, I'm not going to advise the two of you to go back to California and leave this alone."

"We appreciate your help, Agent Devereaux." Sebastian rose and took Mel by the elbow, squeezing hard before she could hurl whatever insult was in her mind. "I've made reservations at the Doubletree. We'll wait for your call."

Satisfied, Devereaux stood and offered a hand.

"I should have spit in it," Mel grumbled a few moments later when they walked out into the torrid Atlanta evening. "The Feebies always treat PIs like mongrel dogs."

"He'll do his job."

"Right." She was distracted enough to let him open the door of the car they'd rented at the airport. "Because some pal of his took a shine to you in Chicago. What did you do up there, anyway?"

"Not enough." Sebastian shut her door and rounded the hood. "I don't suppose you feel like a quiet drink in the hotel bar and a leisurely dinner."

"Not on your life." She snapped her seat belt into place. "I need a pair of binoculars. Must be a sporting goods store around here someplace."

"I imagine I could find one."

"A long-range camera," she said to herself, pushing up the sleeves of her borrowed shirt. "A federal case," she muttered. "Well there's no law that says I can't take a nice drive through the 'burbs, is there?"

"I don't believe there is," Sebastian said as he pulled into traffic. "Perhaps a walk, as well. Nothing quite like a walk in a nice neighborhood on a summer evening."

She turned her head to beam a smile at him. "You're all right, Donovan."

"That kind of flattery will last me a lifetime."

* * *

"Can you—?" Mel bit her lip and swallowed the question as they drove slowly down the tree-lined streets of Forest Park.

"Can I tell which house?" Sebastian finished for her. "Oh, eventually."

"How—?" She cut that thought off, as well, and lifted the binoculars.

"How does it work?" He smiled and turned left, in what appeared to Mel to be an unstudied decision. "That's a bit complicated to explain. Perhaps sometime, if you're still interested, I'll try."

When he pulled over to the curb and stopped, she frowned. "What are you doing?"

"They often walk him here after dinner."

"What?"

"They like to take him out in the stroller after dinner, before his bath."

Before she realized what she meant to do, Mel reached out, put a hand on his cheek to turn his face to hers. She blinked once, stunned by the flash of power in his eyes. How dark they were, she thought. Nearly black. When she managed to speak, her voice was barely a whisper.

"Where is he?"

"In the house across the street. The one with the

blue shutters and the big tree in the front yard." He grabbed her wrist before she could reach for the doorhandle. "No."

"If he's in there, I'm going in and getting him. Damn it, let go of me."

"Think." Because he understood that she would feel long before she would think, he pressed her back against the seat with both hands on her shoulders. No easy task, he thought grimly. She might be as slim as a wand, but she was strong. "Hellfire, Mel, listen to me. He's safe. David's safe. You'll only complicate and confuse things by bursting in there and trying to take him from them."

Her eyes blazed as she strained against him. He thought she looked like a goddess, ready to fling lightning from her fingertips. "They stole him."

"No. No, they didn't. They don't know he was stolen. They think he was given away, or they've convinced themselves he was because they were desperate for a child. Haven't you ever been desperate enough to take a shortcut, to overlook that blurred line and grab what you wanted?"

Furious, she could only shake her head. "He's not their child."

"No." His voice gentled, as did his hold. "But for three months he has been. He's Eric to them, and they love him very much. Enough to pretend he was meant to be theirs."

She struggled to control her breathing. "How can you ask me to leave him with them?"

"Only for a little while longer." He stroked a hand over her cheek. "I swear Rose will have him back before tomorrow night."

She swallowed, nodded. "Let go of me." When he did, she picked up the binoculars with unsteady hands. "You were right to stop me. It's important to be sure."

She focused on the wide bay window, seeing pastel walls through gauzy curtains. She saw a baby swing, and a maroon couch with a clutter of toys scattered over it. With her lips pressed together, Mel watched a woman walk into view. A trim brunette in walking shorts and a cotton blouse. The woman's hair swung prettily as she turned her head to laugh at someone out of sight.

Then she held out her arms.

"Oh, God. David."

Mel's knuckles whitened on the field glasses as she saw a man pass David to the woman's waiting arms. Behind the filmy curtains, she saw David's smile.

"Let's take a walk," Sebastian said quietly, but she shook her head.

"I need some pictures." Hands steady again, Mel

set the glasses aside and took up the camera, with its telescopic lens. "If we can't convince Devereaux to move, maybe these will."

Patiently she took half a roll, waiting when they moved out of view, snapping when they walked in front of the window again. Her chest hurt. There was such terrible pressure there that she rubbed the heel of her hand against it.

"Let's walk." She set the camera down on the floor of the car. "They may bring him out soon."

"If you try to snatch him—"

"I'm not stupid," she told him sharply. "I wasn't thinking before. I know how it needs to be done."

They got out on opposite sides, then rejoined on the sidewalk.

"It might look less conspicuous if you held my hand." Sebastian held his out to hers. She studied it dubiously, then shrugged.

"Wouldn't hurt, I guess."

"You have such a romantic heart, Sutherland." He swung their joined hands up to his lips and kissed her fingers. The rude name she called him only made him smile. "I've always enjoyed neighborhoods like this without ever wanting to live in one. Tidy lawns. A neighbor pruning roses over the fence." He inclined his head toward a young boy speeding down the street on a bike. "Kids out playing. Barbecue smoke, and children's laughter in the air."

She'd always longed for a niche in such a place. Not wanting to admit it to him, or to herself, she shrugged. "Crabgrass. Nosy neighbors spying through the front blinds. Bad-tempered dogs."

As if she'd called it up, one came barreling across a lawn, barking deep in its throat. Sebastian merely turned his head and stared. The dog stumbled to a halt, whimpered a little, then skulked away with his tail between his legs.

Impressed, Mel pursed her lips. "Nice trick."

"It's a gift." Sebastian released her hand and put an arm around her shoulders. "Relax," he murmured. "You don't have to worry about him."

"I'm fine."

"You're tight as a drum. Here." He shifted his hand, moving it to the base of her neck. When Mel felt his fingertips prod gently, she tried to shake him off.

"Look, Donovan—"

"Shhh. It's another gift." He did something, even with her wiggling away. She felt the tensed muscles of her shoulders go fluid.

"Oh," she managed.

"Better?" He tucked her under his arm again. "If

I had more time—God knows, if I had you naked—I'd work all the kinks out." He grinned down into her astonished face. "It seems only fair to let you in on some of my thoughts from time to time. And I have been thinking about getting you naked quite a bit."

Flustered, mortally afraid she might blush, she looked straight ahead. "Well, think about something else."

"It's hard. Particularly when you look so fetching in my shirt."

"I don't like flirtations," she said under her breath.

"My dear Mary Ellen, there's a world of difference between a flirtation and a direct statement of desire. Now, if I were to tell you what lovely eyes you have, how they remind me of the hills in my homeland—that would be flirting. Or if I mentioned that your hair is like the gold in a Botticelli painting, or that your skin is as soft as the clouds that drift over my mountain some evenings—that could be construed as flirting."

There was an odd, distinctly uncomfortable fluttering in her stomach. She wanted it to stop.

"If you said any of those things I'd think you'd lost your mind."

"Which is exactly why I opted for the direct approach. I want you in bed. My bed." Under one of the spreading oaks, he stopped, turning her into his arms before she could so much as sputter. "I want to undress you. Touch you. I want to watch you come alive when I'm inside you." He leaned down to catch her lower lip between his teeth. "And then I want to do it all over again." He felt her shudder and turned the nip into a long, searching kiss. "Direct enough?"

Her hands were against his chest, fingers spread. She had no idea how they'd gotten there. Her mouth felt swollen and stung and hungry. "I think…" But, of course, she couldn't think at all, and that was the problem. Her blood was pounding so hard that she wondered people didn't come out of their houses to see what the racket was about. "You're crazy."

"For wanting you, or for saying it?"

"For…for thinking I'd be interested in a quick tumble with you. I hardly know you."

He caught her chin with his fingers. "You know me." He kissed her again. "And I didn't say anything about quick."

Before she could speak again, he tensed. "They're coming out," he said, without turning around. Over his shoulder she could see the door open and the brunette pushing out a stroller. "Let's cross the street. You can get a good look as they walk by."

She'd tensed up again. Sebastian kept an arm

around her shoulders, as much in warning as in support. She could hear the man and woman talking to each other. It was the light, happy conversation of two young parents with a healthy baby. Their words were nothing but a blur. Without thinking, she slipped an arm around Sebastian's waist and held on.

Oh, he'd grown! She felt tears rush stinging to her eyes and willed them back. He was moving quickly beyond baby to toddler. There were little red hightops on his feet, scuffed, as if he might have been walking already. His hair was longer, curling around his round, rosy face.

And his eyes... She stopped, had to bite back his name. He was looking at her as he rolled along in the bright blue stroller. Looking right at her, and there was a smile, a smile of recognition, in his eyes. He squealed, held out his arms.

"My boy likes pretty women," the man said with a proud grin as they rolled David past.

Rooted to the spot, Mel watched David crane his neck around the stroller, saw his lips move into a pout. He let out a wail of protest that had the woman crooning to him.

"He knew me," Mel whispered. "He remembered me."

"Yes, he did. It's difficult to forget love." He

caught her as she took a stumbling step forward. "Not now, Mel. We'll go call Devereaux."

"He knew me." She found her voice muffled against a cool linen shirt. "I'm all right," she insisted, but she didn't try to break away.

"I know you are." He pressed his lips to her temple, stroked a hand over her hair and waited for her tremors to pass.

It was one of the most difficult things she'd ever done, standing on the sidewalk in front of the house with the blue shutters and the big tree in the yard. Devereaux and a female agent were inside. She'd watched them go in, through the door opened by the young brunette. She'd still been in her robe, Mel remembered, and there had been a flicker of fear, or perhaps knowledge, in her eyes as she bent to retrieve the morning paper.

She could hear weeping now, deep, grieving tears. Her heart wanted to hold rock hard against it, but it couldn't.

When would they come out? Stuffing her hands in her pockets, she paced the sidewalk. It had already been too long. Devereaux had still insisted that they wait until morning, and she'd had hardly a wink of sleep at the hotel. It was well over an hour since they'd gone inside.

"Why don't you sit in the car?" Sebastian suggested.

"I couldn't sit."

"They won't let us take him yet. Devereaux explained the procedure. It'll take hours to do the blood test and the print checks."

"They'll let me stay with him. They'll damn well let me stay with him. He's not going to be with strangers." She pressed her lips together. "Tell me about them," she blurted out. "Please."

He'd expected her to ask, and he turned away from the house to look into Mel's eyes as he told her. "She was a teacher. She resigned when David came to them. It was important to her to spend as much time with him as possible. Her husband is an engineer. They've been married eight years, and have been trying to have a child almost since the start. They're good people, very loving to each other, and with room in their hearts for a family. They were easy prey, Mel."

He could see in her face the war between compassion and fury, between right and wrong. "I'm sorry for them," she whispered. "I'm sorry to know that anyone would exploit that kind of love, that kind of need. I hate what's been done to everyone involved."

"Life isn't always fair."

"Life isn't usually fair," she corrected.

She paced some more, casting dark, desperate looks at the bay window. When the door opened, she shifted to her toes, ready to dash. Devereaux strode toward her.

"The boy knows you?"

"Yes. I told you he recognized me when he saw me yesterday."

He nodded. "He's upset, wailing pretty good, making himself half-sick, what with Mr. and Mrs. Frost carrying on. We've got the woman calming down. Like I told you, we'll have to take the boy in until we can check the matches and clear up the paperwork. Might be easier for him if you went in for him, drove along with Agent Barker."

"Sure." Her heart began to pound in her throat. "Donovan?"

"I'll follow you."

She went inside, fighting to shield her heart and mind from the hopeless weeping beyond a bedroom door. She walked down a hallway, stepping over a plastic rocking horse and into the nursery.

Where the walls were pale blue and painted with sailboats. Where the crib by the window held a circus mobile.

Just as he'd said, she thought as her mouth went dry. Exactly as he'd said.

Then she tossed all that aside and reached down for the crying David.

"Oh, baby." She pressed her face to his, drying his cheeks with her own. "David, sweet little David." She soothed him, brushing his damp hair back from his face, grateful the agent's back was to her so that he couldn't see her own eyes fill.

"Hey, big guy." She kissed his trembling lips. He hiccuped, rubbed his eyes with his fists, then let out a tired sigh as his head dropped to her shoulder. "That's my boy. Let's go home, huh? Let's go home and see Mom and Dad."

## Chapter 7

"I'll never be able to thank you. Never." Rose stood looking out her kitchen window. In the courtyard beyond, her husband and son sat in a patch of sunlight, rolling a bright orange ball around. "Just looking at them makes me…"

"I know." Mel slipped an arm around her shoulders. As they watched in silence, listening to David laugh, Rose brought her hand up to Mel's and squeezed tight. "They look real good out there, don't they?"

"Perfect." Rose dabbed her eyes with a tissue and

sighed. "Just perfect. When I think how afraid I was that I'd never see David again—"

"Then don't think. David's back where he belongs."

"Thanks to you and Mr. Donovan." Rose moved away from the window, but her gaze kept going back to it again and again. Mel wondered how long it would be before Rose would feel comfortable with David out of her sight. "Can you tell me anything about the people who had him, Mel? The FBI were very sympathetic and kind, but…"

"Tight-lipped," Mel finished. "They were good people, Rose. Good people who wanted a family. They made a mistake, trusted someone they shouldn't have trusted. But they took good care of David."

"He's grown so. And he's been trying to take a few steps." There was a bitterness, a sharp tang of bitterness in the back of her throat, at having missed those three precious months of her son's life. But with it was a sorrow for another mother in another city with an empty crib to face. "I know they loved him. And I know how hurt and afraid she must be now. But it's worse for her than it was for me. She knows she'll never have him back." She laid her fisted hands on the counter. "Who did this to us, Mel? Who did this to all of us?"

"I don't know. But I'm working on it."

"Will you work with Mr. Donovan? I know how concerned he is."

"Sebastian?"

"We talked about it a little when he stopped by."

"Oh?" Mel thought she did nonchalance very well. "He came by?"

Rose's face softened. She looked almost as she had in those carefree days before David's abduction. "He brought David his teddy bear, and this cute little blue sailboat."

A sailboat, Mel mused. Yes, he would have thought of that. "That was nice of him."

"He just seemed to understand both sides of it, you know? What Stan and I went through, what those people in Atlanta are going through right now. All because there's someone out there who doesn't care about people at all. Not about babies or mothers or families. He only wants to make money from them." Her lips trembled then firmed. "I guess that's why Mr. Donovan wouldn't let me and Stan pay him anything."

"He didn't take a fee?" Mel asked, struggling to sound disinterested.

"No, he wouldn't take a dime." Recalling other duties, Rose opened the oven to check on her meat loaf. "He said Stan and I should send what we thought we could afford to one of the homeless shelters."

"I see."

"And he said he was going to think about following up on the case."

"The case?"

"He said…something like it wasn't right for babies to be stolen out of cribs and sold off like puppies. That there were some lines you couldn't cross."

"Yes, there are." Mel snatched up her bag. "I have to go, Rose."

Surprised, Rose shut the oven door. "Can't you stay for dinner?"

"I really can't." She hesitated, then did something she rarely did, something she wished she could do with more ease. She kissed Rose's cheek. "There's something I have to take care of."

She supposed she should have done it before. But they'd been back in Monterey for only a couple of days. Mel skimmed through a low-lying cloud on her way up the mountain. It wasn't as if he'd gone out of his way to come and see her, she thought. He'd gone by Rose's apartment, but he hadn't driven a few more blocks to hers.

Obviously he hadn't meant any of that nonsense he'd been spouting about finding her attractive, about wanting her. All that stuff about her eyes and her hair and her skin. Mel drummed her fingers on the gearshift. If he'd meant any of it, he'd have made a move by now. She wished he had. How could she decide if she would block it or not if he didn't bother to make a move?

So she'd beard the wolf in his den. There were obligations to fulfill, statements to be made, and questions to be answered.

Certain she was ready for all of that, Mel turned into Sebastian's bumpy lane. Halfway up she hit the brakes as a horse and rider leapt in front of her. The black stallion and the dark man on his back bounded across the gravel track in a flash of muscle and speed. At the sight of the gleaming horse and the golden-skinned man with his ebony hair flying in the wind, she was tossed back centuries to when there were dragons to be slain and magic sung in the air.

Mel sat openmouthed as they thundered up the rocky slope, through a pocket of mist and back into the stream of sun. No centaur had ever looked more magnificent.

As the echoes of hoofbeats died away, she nudged her car up the lane. This was reality, she reminded herself. The engine groaned and complained at the incline, coughed, sputtered, then finally crept its way up to the house.

As she expected, Sebastian was in the paddock, rubbing Eros down. Dismounted, he looked no less magnificent, no less mystical. Energy and life vibrated from him. The excitement of the ride was still on his face, in his eyes. The strength of it was in the rippling muscles of his back and forearms as he cooled down his mount.

Mel thought that if she touched him now her fingers would burn.

"Nice day for a ride, I guess."

Sebastian looked over Eros's withers and smiled. "Most are. I'm sorry I didn't greet you, but I hate to stop Eros when he has his head."

"It's all right," She was glad he hadn't. Mel was dead certain she wouldn't have managed more than a stutter if he'd spoken to her astride that horse. "I just stopped by to see if you had a few minutes to clear things up."

"I think I could find some time for you." He patted the stallion's left flank, and then, resting the horse's knee on his thigh, began to clean the hoof. "You've seen Rose?"

"Yes, I've just come from there. She said you'd been by. You brought David a sailboat."

Sebastian glanced up, then moved to the next hoof. "I thought it might help ease some of his confusion to have something familiar from those weeks he was away."

"It was very…kind."

He straightened, then moved on to the front leg. "I have my moments."

On more solid ground now, Mel braced a boot on the lowest rung of the fence. "Rose said you wouldn't take a fee."

"I believe I pointed out before that I don't need the money."

"I'm aware of that." Mel leaned on the fence, running her fingers down Eros's neck. Nothing magical there, she assured herself. Just a magnificent beast in his prime. Much like his master. "I did some checking. You have your fingers in a lot of pies, Donovan."

"That's one way of putting it."

"I guess it's easier to make money when you've got a bundle behind you to start with."

He examined the last hoof. "I suppose. And it would follow it would be easier to lose money under the same conditions."

"You got me there." She tilted her head as he straightened again. "That business in Chicago. It was rough."

She saw the change in his face and was sorry for it. This wasn't something he took lightly or brushed off in a matter of days. "It was difficult, yes. Failure is."

"But you helped them find him. Stop him."

"Five lives lost isn't what I term a success." He gave Eros a slap on the rump to send him trotting off. "Why don't you come inside while I clean up?"

"Sebastian."

He knew it was the first time she'd used his given name. It surprised him enough to have him pausing, one hand on the fence, his body poised to vault.

"Five lives lost," she said quietly. Her eyes were dark with understanding. "Do you know how many saved?"

"No." He came over the fence, landing lightly in front of her. "No, I don't. But it helps that you'd ask." He took her arm, his fingers sliding from shoulder to elbow to wrist. "Come inside."

She liked it out here, where there was plenty of room to maneuver. Should maneuvering be necessary. But it seemed foolish and undeniably weak not to go in the house with him.

"There is something I want to talk with you about."

"I assumed there was. Have you had dinner?"

"No."

"Good. We'll talk while we eat."

They went in through the side of the house, climbing onto a redwood deck flanked with pots spilling over with impatiens and going through a wide glass door directly into the kitchen. It was all royal blue and white, and as sleek and glossy as a page out of a high-fashion magazine. Sebastian went directly to a small glass-fronted refrigerator and chose a chilled bottle of wine from a rack inside.

"Have a seat." He gestured to a stool at the tiled work island. After uncorking the wine, he poured her a glass. "I need to clean up," he said, setting the wine on the counter in front of her. "Be at home."

"Sure."

The moment he was out of the room, she was off the stool. Mel didn't consider it rude. It was innate curiosity. There was no better way to find out what made people tick than by poking around their personal space. And she desperately wanted to know what made Sebastian Donovan tick.

The kitchen was meticulously neat, spotless counters and appliances, the dishes in their glass-fronted cupboards arranged according to size. The room didn't smell of detergent or disinfectant, but of…air, she decided, fresh, faintly herb-scented.

There were several clusters of herbs hanging upside down in front of the window over the sink.

Mel sniffed at them, finding their aroma pleasant and vaguely mysterious.

She opened a drawer at random and found baking utensils. She tried another and found more kitchen gadgets neatly stacked.

Where was the clutter? she wondered as she frowned around the room. And the secrets one always found jumbled with it?

Not so much discouraged as intrigued, she slipped back onto the stool and picked up her wine a moment before he came into the room again.

He wore black now—snug coal-colored jeans and a black shirt rolled up to his elbows. His feet were bare. When he picked up the wine to pour his own glass, Mel realized he looked like what he claimed to be.

A wizard.

Smiling, he tapped his glass to hers, leaning close to stare into her eyes. "Will you trust me?"

"Huh?"

His smile widened. "To choose the menu."

She blinked, took a hasty sip of wine. "Sure. I'll eat most anything."

As he began gathering ingredients and pots and pans, she let out a slow, relieved breath. "You're going to cook?"

"Yes. Why?"

"I figured you'd just call out for something." Her brows drew together as he poured oil in a skillet. "It's an awful lot of trouble."

"I enjoy it." Sebastian snipped some herbs into a bowl. "It relaxes me."

Mel scratched her knee and gave the mixture he was making a doubtful look. "You want me to help you?"

"You don't cook."

She lifted a brow. "How do you know?"

"I got a glimpse of your kitchen. Garlic?"

"Sure."

Sebastian crushed the clove with the flat of his knife. "What did you want to talk to me about, Mel?"

"A couple of things." She shifted in her chair, then rested her chin on her hand. Odd, she hadn't realized she would enjoy watching him cook. "Things turned out the way they were supposed to for Rose and Stan and David. What's that you're putting in there?"

"Rosemary."

"It smells good." So did he, she thought. Gone was the sexy leather-and-sweat scent he'd carried with him after the ride. It had been replaced by that equally sexy forest fragrance that was both wild and utterly male. She sipped her wine again, relaxing enough to toe off her boots. "For Mr. and Mrs. Frost back in Georgia, things are pretty awful right now."

Sebastian scooped tomato and garlic and herbs into a skillet. "When someone wins, someone usually loses."

"I know how it works. We did what we had to do, but we didn't finish."

He coated boneless chicken breasts before laying them in a pan. He liked the way she sat there, swinging one leg lazily and watching his culinary preparations with a careful eye. "Go on."

"We didn't get the one who matters, Donovan. The one who arranged the whole thing. We got David back, and that was the most important thing, but we didn't finish. He's not the only baby who's been stolen."

"How do you know?"

"It's logical. An operation that slick, that pat. It wasn't just a one-shot deal."

"No." He topped off their glasses, then poured some of the wine onto the chicken. "It's not."

"So, here's the way I see it." She pushed off the stool. Mel felt she thought better on her feet. "The Frosts had a contact. Now, they might have been able to turn the feds onto him, or he could be long gone. I'd go with long gone." She stopped pacing to tilt her head.

Sebastian nodded. "Continue."

"Okay. It's a national thing. A real company. Got to have a lawyer, someone to handle the adoption papers. Maybe a doctor, too. Or at least someone with connections in the fertility business. The Frosts had all kinds of fertility tests. I checked."

Sebastian stirred and sniffed and checked, but he was listening. "I imagine the FBI checked, as well."

"Sure they did. Our pal Devereaux's right on top of things. But I like to finish what I start. You've got all these couples trying to start a family. They'll try anything. Regulate their sex lives, their diets, dance naked under the full moon. And pay. Pay all kinds of money for tests, for operations, for drugs. And if none of it works, they'll pay for a baby."

She came back to the island to sniff at one of the pots herself. "Good," she murmured. "I know it's usually on the up-and-up. A reputable adoption agency, a reputable lawyer. And, in most cases, it's the right thing. The baby gets a loving home, the bio-logical mother gets a second chance, and the adoptive parents get their miracle. But then you have the slime factor. The sleazeball who always finds a way to make a buck off someone else's tragedy."

"Why don't you put a couple of plates on the table by the window? I'm listening."

"Okay." She puttered around the kitchen, following his instructions for china, for flatware, for napkins, as she continued to theorize. "But this isn't just any penny-ante sleaze. This is a smart one, slick enough to pull together an organization that can snatch a kid from one coast, pass him along like a football cross-country and bounce him into a nice, affluent home thousands of miles away."

"I haven't found anything to argue about yet."

"Well, he's the one we have to get to. They haven't picked up Parkland yet, but I figure they will. He's not a pro. He's just some jerk who tried to find a quick way to pay off a debt and keep his kneecaps intact. He won't be much of a lead when they find him, but he'll be something. I have to figure the feds will keep him under wraps."

"So far your figuring seems flawless. Take the bottle and sit."

She did, curling her legs under her on the corner bench by the window. "It's not likely the feds would cut a PI much of a break."

"No." Sebastian set platters down on the table, pasta curls tanged with tomatoes and herbs, the wine-braised chicken, thick slabs of crusty bread.

"They'd cut you one. They owe you."

Sebastian served Mel himself. "Perhaps."

"They'd give you a copy of Parkland's statement

when they nab him. Maybe even let you talk to him. If you said you were still interested in the case, they'd feed you information."

"Yes, they might." Sebastian sampled the meal and found it excellent. "But am I still interested?"

She clamped a hand over his wrist before he could slice off another bite of tender chicken. "Don't you like to finish what you start?"

He lifted his eyes to hers and looked deep, so deep that her fingers trembled once before they slid away. "Yes, I do."

Uneasy, she broke a piece of bread. "Well, then?"

"I'll help you. I'll use whatever connections I may have."

"I appreciate it." Though she was careful not to touch him again, her lips curved, her eyes warmed. "Really. I'll owe you for this."

"No, I don't think so. Nor will you when you hear my conditions. We'll work together."

She dropped the bread. "Look, Donovan, I appreciate the offer, but I work alone. Anyway, your style—the visions and stuff—it makes me nervous."

"Fair enough. Your style—guns and stuff—makes me nervous. So, we compromise. Work together, deal with each other's…eccentricities. After all, it's the goal that's important, isn't it?"

She mulled it over, poking at the food on her plate. "Maybe I did have an idea that would work better as a couple—a childless couple." Still wary, she glanced up at him. "But if we did agree to compromise, for this one time, we'd have to have rules."

"Oh, absolutely."

"Don't smirk when you say that." With her mind clicking away, she dug into the meal. "This is good." She scooped up another bite. "Really good. It didn't look like all that much trouble."

"You flatter me."

"No, I mean…" She laughed and shrugged and ate some more. "I guess I thought fancy food meant fancy work. My mother worked as a waitress a lot, and she'd bring home all this food from the kitchen. But it was mostly in diners and fast-food joints. Nothing like this."

"Your mother's well?"

"Oh, sure. I got a postcard last week from Nebraska. She travels around a lot. Itchy feet."

"Your father?"

The faintest of hesitations, the briefest shadow of sadness. "I don't remember him."

"How does your mother feel about your profession?"

"She thinks it's exciting—but then, she watches a lot of TV. What about yours?" Mel lifted her glass and gestured. "How do your parents feel about you being the wizard of Monterey?"

"I don't think I'd term it quite that way," Sebastian said after a moment. "But, if they think of it, I imagine they're pleased that I'm carrying on the family tradition."

Mel huffed into her wine. "What are you, like a coven?"

"No," he said gently, unoffended. "We're like a family."

"You know, I wouldn't have believed any of it if I hadn't... Well, I was there. But that doesn't mean I swallow the whole deal." Her eyes flashed up to his, careful and calculating. "I did some reading up, about tests and research and that kind of thing. A lot of reputable scientists believe there's something to psychic phenomena."

"That's comforting."

"Don't be snide," she said, shifting in her seat. "What I mean is, they know they don't completely understand the human mind. That's logical. They look at EEG patterns and EMGs and stuff. You know, they study people who can guess what's on the face of a card without lifting it up, things like that. But that doesn't mean they go in for witchcraft or prophesies or fairy dust."

"A little fairy dust wouldn't hurt you," Sebastian murmured. "I'll have to speak to Morgana about it."

"Seriously," Mel began.

"Seriously." He took her hand. "I was born with elvin blood. I am a hereditary witch who can trace his roots back to Finn of the Celts. My gift is of sight. It was not asked for or demanded, but given. This has nothing to do with logic or science or dancing naked in the moonlight. It is my legacy. It is my destiny."

"Well," Mel said after a long moment. And again: "Well." She moistened her lips and cleared her throat. "In these studies they tested things like telekinesis, telepathy."

"You want proof, Mel?"

"No— Yes. I mean, if we are going to work together on this thing, I'd like to know the extent of your...talent."

"Fair. Think of a number from one to ten. Six," he said before she could open her mouth.

"I wasn't ready."

"But that was the first number that popped into your mind."

It was, but she shook her head. "I wasn't ready." She closed her eyes. "Now."

She was good, he thought. Very good. Right now she was using all her will to block him out. To distract her, he nibbled on the knuckle of the hand he still held. "Three."

She opened her eyes. "All right. How?"

"From your mind to mine." He rubbed his lips over her fingers. "Sometimes in words, sometimes in pictures, sometimes only in feelings that are impossible to describe. Now you're wondering if you had too much wine, because your heart's beating too fast, your skin is warm. Your head's light."

"My head's fine." She jerked her hand from his. "Or it would be if you'd stay out of it. I can feel…"

"Yes." Content, he sat back and lifted his glass. "I know you can. It's very rare, without a blood connection, for anyone to feel me, particularly on such a light scan. You have potential, Sutherland. If you care to explore it, I'd be happy to assist you."

She couldn't quite mask the quick shudder that passed through her. "No, thanks. I like my head just the way it is." Experimentally she put a hand to it while watching Sebastian. "I don't like the idea of anybody being able to read my mind. If we're going to go through with this temporary partnership, that's the number one rule."

"Agreed. I won't look inside your mind unless you ask me to." Noting the doubt in her eyes, he smiled. "I don't lie, Mel."

"Witch's creed?"

"If you like."

She didn't, but she would take him at his word. "Okay, next—we share all information. No holding back."

His smile was both charming and dangerous. "I'm more than willing to agree we've held back long enough."

"We're professional. We keep it professional."

"When appropriate." He touched the rim of his glass to hers. "Is sharing a meal considered professional?"

"We don't have to be ridiculous. What I mean is, if we're going to go under posing as a married couple wanting a child, we don't let the act—"

"Blur those lines of yours," he finished for her. "I understand. Do you have a plan?"

"Well, it would help if we had the cooperation of the FBI."

"Leave that to me."

She grinned. It was exactly what she'd hoped for. "With them backing us up, we can establish a solid identity. Papers, backgrounds, IRS files, the works. We need to come to the attention of the organization, so we'll have to be affluent, but not so high-profile as to scare them off. We should be new in the community we choose. No ties, no family. We'll have to be put on the waiting list of several reputable adoption agencies. Have records from fertility clinics and doctors. Once they've gotten to Parkland or one of the others, we'll have a better idea where to set up, and how."

"There might be an easier way."

"What?"

He waved her aside. "I'll get to it. This could take quite a lot of time."

"It could. It would be worth it."

"We compromise. I work out where we begin, when and how, you handle the procedure from there."

She hesitated, aware she'd never be any good at compromise. "If you pick the when, where and how, it has to be for solid reasons, and I have to accept them."

"All right."

"All right." It seemed simple enough. If there was a frisson of excitement working through her, it was the anticipation of an interesting and rewarding job. "I guess I could help you deal with all these dishes."

She rose, started to stack the delicate china with the competence her waitress mother had taught her. Sebastian put a hand on her arm. The frisson erupted into a flare.

"Leave them."

"You cooked," she said, and strode quickly to the sink. A little room, she thought. A little room and some busywork was all she needed to stay on an even keel. "And from the looks of this kitchen, you're not the type who leaves dirty dishes hanging around."

He was behind her when she turned, and his hands came to her shoulders to prevent her from dodging away. "So, I'll be unpredictable."

"Or you could hire some elves to scrub up," she muttered.

"I don't employ any elves—in California." When her look sharpened, he began to knead her shoulders. "You're tensing up on me, Mel. During dinner you were quite relaxed. You even smiled at me several times, which I found a very pleasant change."

"I don't like people touching me." But she didn't move away. After all, there was nowhere to go.

"Why not? It's merely another form of communication. There are many. Voices, eyes, hands." His slid over her shoulders, turning the muscles there to water. "Minds. A touch doesn't have to be dangerous."

"It can be."

His lips curved as his fingers skimmed down her back. "But you're no coward. A woman like you meets a dangerous situation head-on."

Her chin came up, as he'd known it would. "I came here to talk to you."

"And we've talked." He nudged her closer so that he had only to bend his head to press his lips to the faint cleft in the center of that strong chin. "I enjoyed it."

She would not be seduced. She was a grown woman with a mind of her own, and seduction was, always had been, out of the question. She lifted a hand to his chest, where it lay, fingers spread, neither resisting or inviting.

"I didn't come to play games."

"Pity." His lips hovered a breath from hers before he tilted his head and brushed them under her jaw. "I also enjoy games. But we can save them for another time."

It was becoming very difficult to breathe. "Look, maybe I'm attracted to you, but that doesn't mean...anything."

"Of course not. Your skin's unbelievably delicate just here, Mary Ellen. It's as if your pulse would bruise the flesh if it continued to beat so hard."

"That's ridiculous."

But when he tugged her shirt free of her waistband to let his hands roam up her back, she felt as delicate as a dandelion puff. With a sound that was somewhere between a moan and a sigh, she arched back against him.

"I'd nearly lost my patience," he murmured against her throat. "Waiting for you to come to me."

"I didn't. I haven't." But her arms had wound around him, and her fingers were tangled in his hair. "This isn't why I'm here."

But hadn't she known? Somewhere inside, hadn't she known?

"I have to think. This could be a mistake." But even as she said it, her mouth was moving hungrily over his. "I hate to make mistakes."

"Mmm… Who doesn't?" He cupped his hands under her hips. With a murmur of acceptance, she scooted up, wrapping her legs around his waist. "This isn't one."

"I'll figure it out later," she said as he carried her out of the kitchen. "I really don't want this to mess up the other business. It's too important. I want that to work, I really want that to work, and I'd hate myself if I messed it up just because…"

On a groan, she pressed her mouth to his throat. "I want you. I want you so much."

Her words started a drumbeat in his head, slow, rhythmic, seductive. He dragged her head back with one hand so that he could plunder her mouth. "One has nothing to do with the other."

"It could." She rocked against him as he started up

the steps. Her breath was already coming in pants as her eyes met his. "It should."

"Then so be it." He kicked open the door to the bedroom. "Let's break some rules."

# Chapter 8

She had never been one to throw caution to the winds. To take risks, certainly, but always knowing the consequences. There was no way to figure the odds now, not with him. Again, it was up to instinct. Although her head told her to cut her losses and run, something else, something closer to the bone, urged her to stay.

To trust.

She was still wrapped around him, throbbing at every point a pulse could beat. It wasn't shyness that had her hesitating. She had never considered herself overly sexual or more than average in looks, so she felt she had nothing to be shy about. It was a sudden certainty that this was vital that had her taking one last long look at him.

And what she saw was exactly what she wanted.

Her lips curved slowly. When she started to slide down him, he braced her back against the bedpost so that when her feet touched the floor she was trapped between the smooth, carved wood and his body.

His eyes stayed on hers as his hands moved slowly upward, fingertips sliding over thighs, hips, the sides of her breasts, her throat, temples. She shuddered once before his fists closed, viselike, in her hair and his mouth crushed down on hers.

His body was pressed against her so truly that she felt every line and curve. She sensed that the power inside it was that of a wolf on a leash, ready to tear free. But it was his mouth that drove her mind to the edge of reason. Insatiable and possessive, it drew from hers every nuance of emotion. Desires and doubts, fears and longings. She felt her will being passed to him like a gift.

He felt that instant of surrender, when her body was both limp and firm against his, when her lips trembled, then sought more of what he wanted to give. The hunger sliced through him like a silver blade, cleaving the civilized from the desperate and leaving him quivering like a stallion that scents his mate.

He reared his head back, and she saw that his eyes were dark as midnight, full of reckless needs and heedless wants. And power. She trembled, first in fear, then again, in glorious delight.

It was that answer he saw. And it was that answer he took.

With one violent swipe, he tore her shirt to tatters. Her gasp was muffled against his mouth. Even as they tumbled onto the bed, his hands were everywhere, bruising and stroking, taking and tormenting.

In answer she dragged at his shirt, popping buttons, rending seams, as they rolled over the sheets. When she felt his flesh against hers, she let out a long, breathless sigh of approval.

He gave her little time to think, and none to question. He was riding her into a storm filled with thunderclaps and flashing lights and howling winds. She knew it was physical. There was nothing magical about the skill of his hands, the drugging taste of his mouth. But oh, it seemed like magic to be whisked away, beyond the ordinary, beyond even the simple beauty of a rosy dusk and the stirrings of night birds just waking.

Where he took her was all dazzling speed and unspeakable pleasure. A whisper of some language she couldn't understand. An incantation? Some lover's promise? The sound alone was enough to seduce her. A touch, rough or gentle, was accepted with delight. The taste of him, hot and salty on her lips, cool and soothing on her tongue, was enough to make her ravenous for more.

So generous, his hazy mind thought. So strong, so giving. In the lowering light her skin was gilded like a warrior goddess's prepared for battle. She was slim and straight, agile as a fantasy, responsive as a wish. He felt her strangled gasp against his ear, the sudden convulsive dig of her nails into his back as her body shuddered from the climax he gave her.

Even as her limp hand slid from his damp shoulder he was racing over her again. Wild to taste, crazed to make her blood pump hot again until he could hear her breath rasping out his name.

He braced over her, shaking his head until his vision cleared, until he could see her face, her eyes half-closed and drugged with pleasure, her lips swollen from his and trembling on each breath.

"Come with me," he told her.

As her arms encircled, he drove himself inside her. And he knew, as they raced together, that some spells require nothing more than a willing heart.

* * *

She thought she heard music. Lovely, soothing. Heart music. Mel didn't know where the phrase had come from, but she smiled at the thought of it and turned.

There was no one to turn to.

Instantly awake, she sat up in the dark. Though the night was ink black, she knew she was alone in the room. Sebastian's room. Being with him had been no dream. Nor was being alone now a dream.

She groped for the light beside the bed and shielded her eyes until they had adjusted.

She didn't call out his name. It would have made her feel foolish to speak it in an empty bed in a shadowy room. Instead she scrambled up, found his shirt crumpled on the floor. Tugging her arms through the sleeves, she followed the music.

It came from no real direction. Though soft as a whisper, it seemed to surround her. Odd, no matter how she strained to hear, she couldn't be sure if she was hearing voices raised in song, or strings, flutes, horns. It was simply sound, a lovely vibration on the air that was both eerie and beautiful.

She flowed with it, following instinct. The sound grew no louder, no softer, but it did seem to become more fluid, washing over her skin, sliding into her mind as she followed a corridor that snaked left, then climbed a short flight of stairs.

She saw the glow of candlelight, an ethereal flicker that built to a golden flood as she approached a room at the end of the hallway. There was a scent of warm wax, of sandalwood, of pungent smoke.

She wasn't aware she was holding her breath when she stopped in the doorway and looked.

The room wasn't large. She thought the word *chamber* would be more appropriate, but she wasn't sure why such a quaint term came to mind. The walls were a pale, warm-toned wood, burnished now with the mystical lights of dozens of slim white candles.

There were windows, three in the shape of crescent moons. She remembered seeing them from the outside and realized that the room was at the topmost part of the house, facing the cliffs and the sea.

Above, a twinkling of stars could be seen through the skylights he'd opened to the night and the air. There were chairs and tables and stands, all of them looking as if they belonged in some medieval castle, rather than a modern home in Big Sur. On them she saw orbs of crystal, colorful bowls, scribed silver mirrors, slender wands of clear glass, and goblets encrusted with glittering stones.

She didn't believe in magic. Mel knew there was always a false drawer in the magician's chest and an ace of hearts up his sleeve. But standing there, in the doorway of that room, she felt the air pulse and throb as if it were alive with a thousand hearts.

And she knew that there was more, here in this world she thought she knew, than she had ever dreamed of.

Sebastian sat in the center of the room, in the center of a silver pentagram inlaid in the wooden floor. His back was to her, and he was very still. Her curiosity had always been strong, but she discovered something stronger—her need to give him his privacy.

But, even as she stepped back from the doorway, he spoke to her.

"I didn't mean to wake you."

"You didn't." She toyed with one of the few buttons left on his shirt. "The music did. Or I woke up and heard it, and wondered…" She looked around, baffled. She could see no recording device, no stereo. "I wondered where it was coming from."

"The night." He rose. Though she'd never considered herself a prude, she found herself flushing when he stood naked in the candlelight, holding a hand out for her.

"I'm naturally nosy, but I didn't mean to intrude."

"You didn't." Her hesitation had him lifting a brow, then stepping forward to take her hand. "I needed to clear my mind. I couldn't do it beside you." He brought her palm to his lips, pressing them at the center. "Too many thoughts clouding the issue."

"I guess I should've gone home."

"No." He leaned down to kiss her, lightly, sweetly. "No, indeed."

"Well, the thing is…" She backed away a little, wishing she had something to do with her hands. "I don't usually do this sort of thing."

She looked so young, he thought, and so frail, standing there in his shirt, with her hair mussed from love and sleep, and her eyes too wide.

"Should I say that, since you decided to make an exception with me, you do this sort of thing very well?"

"You don't have to." Then her lips turned up. She had done well. They had done incredibly well. "But I don't guess it hurts. Do you usually sit naked on the floor in candlelight?"

"When the spirit moves me."

More comfortable now, she began moving around the room, picking up objects. Lips pursed, she examined a centuries-old scrying mirror. "Is this supposed to be magic stuff?"

In that moment, watching her peer suspiciously at the priceless antiques, he adored her. "That was said to belong to Ninian."

"Who?"

"Ah, Sutherland, your education is sadly lacking. Ninian was a sorceress, reputed to have imprisoned Merlin in his cave of crystal."

"Yeah?" She took a closer look, found it a pretty piece, then set it down to study a globe of smoky quartz. "So what do you use this stuff for?"

"Enjoyment." He had no need for scrying mirrors or crystal balls in order to see. He kept them around him out of an appreciation of tradition and a sense of aesthetics. It amused him to see her frown and squint at the tools of power.

There was something he wanted to give her, a small gift. He hadn't forgotten the fleeting sadness he'd seen in her eyes when she'd told him she didn't remember her father.

"Would you like to see?"

"See what?"

"To see," he said gently, and walked to her. "Come." He took the globe in one hand, her fingers in the other, and drew her back to the center of the room.

"I don't really think—"

"Kneel." He nudged her down with him. "Past or future, Mel? Which would you like?"

With a nervous laugh, she settled back on her heels. "Aren't you supposed to be wearing a turban?"

"Use your imagination." He touched a hand to her cheek. "The past, I think. You prefer taking care of your own future."

"You got that right, but—"

"Put your hands on the globe, Mel. There's nothing to be afraid of."

"I'm not afraid." She squirmed a little, let out a long breath. "It's just a piece of glass. It's weird, that's all," she muttered as she took the crystal. Sebastian put his hands under hers and smiled.

"My aunt Bryna, Morgana's mother, gave me this ball as a christening gift. It was, for me, somewhat like training wheels on a bicycle."

It was cool in her hands, smooth and as cool as lake water. "I had this ball when I was a kid. A black plastic one. You were supposed to ask it questions, then you could shake it and this writing would float up toward this opening. It usually said something like, answer unclear, try again."

Again he smiled, finding her nerves endearing. The power was flowing into him, sweet as wine, easy as a spring breeze. This was a simple thing he would show her. "Look inside," he said, and his voice echoed oddly in the small room. "And see."

She was compelled to do so. At first she saw only a pretty ball with internal fractures glinting rainbows back at her. Then there were shadows, shadows within shadows, forms shifting, colors bleeding.

"Oh," she murmured, for the glass was no longer cool, but as warm as a sunbeam.

"Look," he said again, and it seemed his voice was inside her head. "With your heart."

She saw her mother first, but young, so young, and brightly pretty, despite the heavy use of eyeliner and a lipstick several shades too pale. It was the laughter in her face that brought the prettiness through the cosmetics. Her hair was blond, shoulder-length and straight as a pin. She was laughing at a young man in a white uniform, a sailor's cap perched jauntily on his head.

The man was holding a child of about two who was dressed in a frilly pink dress with black strapped shoes and lacy white socks.

Not just any child, Mel thought as her heart thudded in her throat. Me. The child is me.

In the background was a ship, a big gray naval vessel. There was a band playing something rousingly military, and there were people milling about, talking all at once. She couldn't hear the words, only the sounds.

She saw the man toss her in the air, toss her high. In the candlelit room her stomach leaped and dropped giddily. And here was love and trust and innocence. His eyes beaming up at her with pride and humor and excitement. Strong hands around her. A whiff of after-shave. A giggly laugh tickling her throat as she was caught close.

She watched the images shift. Saw her parents kiss. Oh, the sweetness of it. Then the boy who had been her father gave them a jaunty salute, tossed his duffel bag over his shoulder and walked toward the ship.

The ball in her hand was only pretty glass with inner fractures glinting rainbows back at her.

"My father." Mel might have dropped the globe if Sebastian's hands hadn't held firm. "It was my father. He…he was in the Navy. He wanted to see the world. He left that day from Norfolk. I was only two, I don't remember. My mother said we went down to see him off, and that he'd been excited."

Her voice broke, and she gave herself a minute. "A few months later there was a storm in the Mediterranean, and he was lost at sea. He was only twenty-two. Just a boy, really. She has pictures, but you can't tell from pictures." Mel stared into the globe again, then slowly looked up at Sebastian. "I have his eyes. I never realized I have his eyes."

She closed them a moment, waiting until her system leveled a bit. "I did see it, didn't I?"

"Yes." He lifted a hand to her hair. "I didn't show you to make you sad, Mary Ellen."

"It didn't. It made me sorry." On a sigh, she opened her eyes again. "Sorry I can't remember him. Sorry that my mother remembers too much and that I never understood that before. And it made me happy to have seen him, and them together—all of us together—even once." She slipped her hands away, leaving the ball in his. "Thank you."

"It was a small thing, after what you brought me tonight."

"What I brought?" she asked as he rose to replace the ball.

"Yourself."

"Oh, well..." Clearing her throat, she got to her feet. "I don't know if I'd put it like that."

"How would you put it?"

She looked back at him and felt that new helpless fluttering in her stomach. "I don't know, exactly. We're both adults."

"Yes." He started toward her, and she surprised herself by edging back.

"Unattached."

"So it seems."

"Responsible."

"Admirably." He danced his fingers over her hair. "I've wanted to see you in candlelight, Mary Ellen."

"Don't start that." She brushed his hand away.

"What?"

"Don't call me Mary Ellen, and don't start that violin-and-candlelight business."

His eyes stayed on hers as he trailed a finger down her throat. "You object to romance?"

"Not object, exactly." Her emotions were too close to the surface, much too close, after what she had seen in the globe. She needed to make certain they had their ground rules. "I just don't need it. I don't know what to do with it. And I think we'll deal better if we know where we stand."

"Where do we stand?" he asked, slipping his hands around her waist.

"Like I said, we're responsible, unattached adults. And we're attracted to each other."

He touched his lips to her temple. "So far I find nothing to argue about."

"And as long as we handle this relationship sensibly—"

"Oh, we may run into trouble there."

"I don't see why."

He skimmed his hands up her rib cage until his thumbs circled her nipples. "I don't feel particularly sensible."

Her knees buckled. Her head fell back. "It's just a matter of…establishing priorities."

"I have my priorities." He teased her lips apart with his tongue. "Top of the list is making love with you until we're both a puddle of useless flesh."

"Good." She went willingly when he pulled her to the floor. "Good start."

She really worked better with lists. By the following evening, Mel was huddled at her desk, doing her best to put one together. It was the first free hour she'd had since speeding away from Sebastian's house at 10:00 a.m., already frazzled and behind schedule.

She was never behind schedule. Of course, she'd never had an affair with a witch before. It was obviously a month for firsts.

If she hadn't had an appointment, paperwork and a court appearance waiting, she might not have left his house at all. He'd certainly done everything in his power to discourage her, she remembered, tapping her pencil against her smiling lips.

The man definitely had a lot of power.

But work was work, she reminded herself. She had a business to run.

The best news of the day was that the New Hampshire State Police had picked up James T. Parkland. And there was a certain sergeant, grateful for her tip and annoyed with the federal takeover, who was being very cooperative.

He'd faxed Mel a copy of Parkland's statement on the sly.

It was a start.

She had the name of the high roller who'd held Parkland's IOU, and she intended to put it to good use. With any luck, she'd be spending a few days in Lake Tahoe.

She needed to bring Devereaux around. He'd want to use his own agents on any kind of a sting, and she had to come up with several solid reasons why she and Sebastian would make better bait.

Her assistance and cooperation in the Merrick case would work in her favor, but Mel didn't think it would swing the deal. Her record was good, she didn't do flashy work—and she sensed that Devereaux would disapprove of a hotdogging PI. Her partnership with Sebastian was in her favor, as well. And the fact that she was perfectly willing to let the feds take the lion's share of credit for the collar would add a little weight to her side of the scales.

"Open for business?" Sebastian asked as he pushed open the door.

She struggled to ignore the quick, giddy fluttering in her stomach, and she smiled. "Actually, I'm closing for the day in five minutes."

"Then my timing's good. What's this?" Taking her hand, he pulled her to her feet to examine the trim peach-colored suit she wore.

"Court appearance late this afternoon." She moved her shoulders restlessly as he toyed with the pearls at her throat. "Divorce case. Kind of nasty. So you want to go in looking as much like a lady as possible."

"You succeeded."

"Easy for you to say. It takes twice as much time and trouble to dress like a lady as it does to dress like a normal person." She rested a hip on the desk and handed him a sheet of paper. "I got a copy of Parkland's statement."

"Quick work."

"As you can see, he's a pretty pathetic type. He was desperate. He didn't mean to hurt anybody. He was over his head. Gambling problem. Afraid for his life." She gave a quick, unladylike opinion of his excuses. "I'm surprised he didn't toss out how his father had traumatized him by not giving him a little red wagon for Christmas."

"He'll pay," Sebastian said. "Pathetic or not."

"Right, because he was also stupid. Taking David across the state line really upped the ante." She kicked off her shoes and rubbed her calf with her foot. "Now he claims he got the offer of the job over the phone."

"Sounds reasonable."

"Sure. Want a drink?"

"Mmm." Sebastian read over the statement again while she moved into the kitchen.

"Five thousand dollars for snatching a kid. Pretty paltry, compared with the sentence he's facing. So." She turned, found Sebastian in the doorway and offered him a soft drink. "He owes thirty-five hundred to this casino up in Tahoe, and he knows if he doesn't make a payment soon, he's going to have his face rearranged in a way that might not be pleasing. So he scouts out a kid."

He was following her, but Sebastian was also interested in her personal habitat. "Why David?" he asked as he walked past her into the adjoining room.

"I looked into that. Stan worked on his car about five months ago. Stan'll show off pictures of David to anyone who doesn't run for cover. So when

Parkland figured snatching a kid was better than plastic surgery the hard way, he figured a mechanic's kid might be the ticket. David's cute. Even a sleaze like Parkland would have realized a pretty baby makes an impression on a buyer."

"Um-hmm." Sebastian rubbed a hand over his chin as he studied her bedroom. He assumed it was a bedroom, as there was a narrow, unmade bed in the center of it. It also appeared to be a living room, as it also had an overstuffed chair piled with books and magazines, a portable TV on a wobbly plant stand, and a lamp in the shape of a trout. "Is this where you live?"

"Yeah." She kicked a pair of boots out of the way. "Maid's year off. And so," she continued, dropping down on a chest decorated with stickers of most, if not all, of the fifty states, "he took the job, got all his instructions from Mr. X over the phone. Met the redhead at the prearranged drop and exchanged David for an envelope of cash."

"What's this?"

Mel glanced over. "It's a Bullwinkle bank. Didn't you ever watch Bullwinkle?"

"I believe I did," Sebastian mused, shaking the moose before setting it aside again. "Hokey smokes."

"That's the one. Anyway—"

"And this?" He gestured to a poster tacked to the wall.

"Underdog. Wally Cox used to do the voice. Are you paying attention to me?"

He turned and smiled. "I'm riveted. Do you know it takes a bold soul to mix purple and orange in one room?"

"I like bright colors."

"And red striped sheets."

"They were on sale," she said impatiently. "You turn the light off when you sleep, anyway. Look, Donovan, how long are we going to discuss my decor?"

"Only a moment or two." He picked up a bowl shaped like the Cheshire cat. She'd tossed odds and ends into it. A straight pin, a safety pin, a couple of loose buttons, a .22 bullet, a coupon for the soft drinks she seemed to live on, and what looked to Sebastian to be a lock pick.

"You're not the tidy sort, are you?"

"I use up my organizational talents in business."

"Um-hmm." He set the bowl down and picked up a book. "*The Psychic Handbook?*"

"Research," she said, and scowled. "I got it out of the library a couple of weeks ago."

"What did you think?"

"I think it has very little to do with you."

"I'm sure you're right." He set it aside again. "This room has very much to do with you. Just as that streamlined office out there does. Your mind is very disciplined, like your file cabinet."

She wasn't sure if it was a compliment or not, but she recognized the look in his eye. "Look, Donovan…"

"But your emotions," he continued, moving toward her, "are very chaotic, very colorful."

She batted his hand away when he toyed with her pearls. "I'm trying to have a professional conversation."

"You closed up shop for the day. Remember?"

"I don't have regular hours."

"Neither do I." He flipped open a button of her suit jacket. "I've been thinking about making love with you ever since I finished making love with you this morning."

Her skin was going hot, and she knew her attempts to stop him from undoing her jacket were halfhearted at best. "You must not have enough on your mind."

"Oh, you're quite enough. I have started on some arrangements that should please you. Professionally."

She turned her head just in time to avoid his mouth. "What arrangements?"

"A long conversation with Agent Devereaux and his superior."

Her eyes flew open again as she struggled away from his hands. "When? What did they say?"

"You could say the stew's simmering. It'll take a couple of days. You'll have to be patient."

"I want to talk to him myself. I think he should—"

"You'll have your shot at him tomorrow. The next day, at the latest." He drew her hands behind her back, handcuffing her wrists with his fingers. "What's going to happen will happen soon enough. I know the when, I know the where."

"Then—"

"Tonight, it's just you and me."

"Tell me—"

"I'm going to show you," he murmured. "Show you just how easy it is to think of nothing else, to feel nothing else. To want nothing else." With his eyes on hers, he teased her mouth. "I wasn't gentle with you before."

"It doesn't matter."

"I don't regret it." He nipped lightly at her lower lip, then soothed the small pain with his tongue. "It's just that seeing you tonight, in your quiet little suit, makes me want to treat you like a lady. Until it drives you crazy."

Her laugh was breathless as his tongue danced up her throat. "I think you already are."

"I haven't even started."

With his free hand, he nudged the jacket from her shoulder. She wore a sheer pastel blouse underneath that made him think of summer teas and formal garden parties. While his mouth roamed over her face and throat, he traced his fingers over the sheer cloth and the lace beneath.

Her body was already quivering. She thought it ridiculous that he held her arms captive, that she allowed it. But there was a dreamy excitement at having him touch her this way, slowly, experimentally, thoroughly.

She felt his breath against her flesh as he opened her blouse, and the moist warmth of his tongue cruising over the tops of her breast just above, then just beneath, the chemise. She knew she was still standing, her feet on the floor, her legs pressed back against the bed, but it felt like floating. Floating, while he lazily savored her as if she were a banquet to be sampled at his whim.

Her skirt slithered down her legs. His hand trailed up. Her murmur of approval was low and long as his fingers toyed seductively with the hook of her garter.

"So unexpected, Mary Ellen." With one expert flick, he unsnapped the front.

"Practical," she said on a gasp as his fingers skimmed up toward the heat. "Cheaper this way, because I'm always…running them."

"Delightfully practical."

Struggling against the need to rush, he laid her back on the bed. In the name of Finn, how could he have known that the sight of that strong, angular body in bits of lace would rip his self-control to shreds?

He wanted to devour, to conquer, to possess.

But he had promised her some tenderness.

He knelt over her, lowered his mouth to hers, and kept his word.

And he was right. In mere moments she understood he was so very right. It was easy to think of nothing but him. To feel nothing but him. To want nothing but him.

She was rocked in the cradle of his gentleness, her body as alive as it had been the night before, certainly as desired as it had been but with the added aspect of being treasured for a femininity she so often forgot.

He savored her, and sent her gliding. He explored and showed her new secrets of herself. All the rush and fury they had indulged in the night before had shifted focus. Now the world was slow, the air was soft, and passion was languid.

And when she felt his heart thudding wildly

against hers, when his murmurs became urgent, breathless, she understood that he was as seduced as she by what they made together.

She opened for him, drawing him in, heat to heat, pulse to pulse. When his body shuddered, it was she who cradled him.

## Chapter 9

"We're wasting time."

"On the contrary," Sebastian said, pausing at a shop window to examine an outfit on a stylized, faceless mannequin. "What we're doing is basic, even intricate, groundwork for the operation."

"Shopping?" She made a disgusted sound and hooked her thumbs in her front pockets. "Shopping for an entire day?"

"My dear Sutherland, I'm quite fond of the way you look in jeans, but as the wife of an affluent businessman you need a more extensive wardrobe."

"I've already tried on enough stuff to clothe three women for a year. It'll take a tractor-trailer to deliver it all to your house."

He gave her a bland look. "It was easier to convince the FBI to cooperate than it is you."

Because that made her feel ungrateful and petty, she squirmed. "I'm cooperating. I've been cooperating for hours. I just think we have enough."

"Not quite." He gestured toward the dress in the display. "Now this would make a statement."

Mel chewed on her lower lip as she studied it. "It has sequins."

"You have religious or political objections to sequins?"

"No. It's just that I'm not the glittery type. I'd feel like a jerk. And there's hardly anything to it." She flicked her gaze over the tiny strapless black dress, which left the mannequin's white legs bare to midthigh. "I don't see how you could sit down in it."

"I seem to recall a little number you wore to go to a bar a few weeks ago."

"That was different. I was working." At his patient, amused look, she grimaced. "Okay, okay, Donovan, you made your point."

"Be a good soldier," he said, and patted her cheek. "Go in and try it on."

She grumbled and muttered and swore under her breath, but she was a good soldier. Sebastian roamed the boutique, selecting accessories and thinking of her.

She didn't give a hang for fashion, he mused, and was more embarrassed than pleased that she could now lay claim to a wardrobe most woman would envy. She would play her part, and play it well. She would wear the clothes he'd selected and be totally oblivious to the fact that she looked spectacular in them.

As soon as it was possible, she would slip back into her jeans and boots and faded shirts. And be equally oblivious to the fact that she looked equally spectacular in them.

By Merlin's beard, you have it bad, Donovan, he thought as he chose a silver evening bag with an emerald clasp. His mother had once told him that love was more painful, more delightful and more unstoppable when it came unexpectedly.

How right she had been.

The last thing he'd expected was to feel anything more than an amused attraction for a woman like Mel. She was tough, argumentative, prickly and radically independent. Hardly seductive qualities in a woman.

She was also warm and generous, loyal and brave, and honest.

What man could resist an acid-tongued woman with a caring heart and a questing mind? Certainly not Sebastian Donovan.

It would take time and patience to win her over completely. He didn't have to look to know. She was much too cautious—and, despite her cocky exterior, too insecure—to hand over her heart with both hands until she was sure of its reception.

He had time, and he had patience. If he didn't look to be sure, it was because he felt it would be unfair to both of them. And because, in a deep, secret chamber of his own heart, he was afraid he would look and see her walking away.

"Well, I got it on," Mel griped behind him. "But I don't see how it's going to stay up for long."

He turned. And stared.

"What is it?" Alarmed, she slapped a hand to the slight swell of her breasts above the glittery sequins and looked down. "Do I have it on backwards or something?"

The laugh did the trick of starting his heart again. "No. You wear it very well. There's nothing that raises a man's blood pressure as quickly as a long, slim woman in a black dress."

She snorted. "Give me a break."

"Perfect, perfect." The saleswoman came over to

pluck and peck. Mel rolled her eyes at Sebastian. "It fits like a dream."

"Yes," he agreed. "Like a dream."

"I have some red silk evening pants that would be just darling on her."

"Donovan," Mel began, a plea in her voice, but he was already following the eager clerk.

Thirty minutes later, Mel strode out of the store. "That's it. Case closed."

"One more stop."

"Donovan, I'm not trying on any more clothes. I'd rather be staked to an anthill."

"No more clothes," he promised.

"Good. I could be undercover on this case for a decade and not wear everything."

"Two weeks," he told her. "It won't take longer than two weeks. And by the time we've made the rounds at the casinos, the clubs, attended a few parties, you'll have made good use of the wardrobe."

"Two weeks?" She felt excitement begin to percolate through the boredom. "Are you sure?"

"Call it a hunch." He patted her hand. "I have a feeling that what we do in Tahoe will be enough to set the dominoes tumbling on this black-market operation."

"You never told me exactly how you convinced the feds to let us go with this."

"I have a history with them. You could say I called in a few favors, made some promises."

She stopped to look in another store window, not to peruse the wares, but because she needed a moment to choose her words. "I know I couldn't have gotten them to back me without you. And I know that you don't really have a stake in any of this."

"I have the same stake as you." He turned her to face him. "You don't have a client, Sutherland. No retainer, no fee."

"That doesn't matter."

"No." He smiled and kissed her brow. "It doesn't. Sometimes you're involved simply because there's a chance you can make a difference."

"I thought it was because of Rose," Mel said slowly. "And it is, but it's also because of Mrs. Frost. I can still hear the way she was crying when we took David away."

"I know."

"It's not that I'm a do-gooder," she said, suddenly embarrassed. He kissed her once more.

"I know. There are rules." He took her hand, and they began to walk again.

She took her time, keeping her voice light, as she touched on something that had been nagging at her brain for days.

"If we can really get set up by the end of the week, we'll be sort of living together for a while."

"Does that bother you?"

"Well, no. If it doesn't bother you." She was beginning to feel like a fool, but it was important she make him understand she wasn't the kind of woman who mixed fantasy with reality. "We'll be pretending that we're married. That we're in love and everything."

"It's convenient to be in love when you're married."

"Right." She let out a huff of breath. "I just want you to know that I can play the game. I can be good at it. So you shouldn't think that…"

He toyed with her fingers as they walked. "Shouldn't think what?"

"Well, I know that some people can get carried away, or mix up the way things are with the way they're pretending they are. I just don't want you to get nervous that I'd do that."

"Oh, I think my nerves can stand the pretense of you being in love with me."

He said it so lightly that she scowled down at the sidewalk. "Well, good. Fine. Just so we know where we stand."

"I think we should practice." He whipped her around so that she collided with him.

"What?"

"Practice," he repeated. "So we can be sure you can pull off the role of the loving wife." He held her a little closer. "Kiss me, Mary Ellen."

"We're out on the street. We're in public."

"All the more reason. It hardly matters how we behave privately. You're blushing."

"I am not."

"You certainly are, and you'll have to watch that. I don't think it would embarrass you to kiss a man you've been married to for—what is it? Five years. And, according to our established cover, we lived together a full year before that. You were twenty-two when you fell in love with me."

"I can add," she muttered.

"You wash my socks."

Her lips quirked. "The hell I do. We have a modern marriage. You do the laundry."

"Ah, but you've given up your career as an ad executive to make a home."

"I hate that part." She slipped her arms around his neck. "What am I supposed to do all day?"

"Putter." He grinned. "Initially, we'll be on vacation, establishing our new home. We'll spend a lot of time in bed."

"Well, all right." She grinned back. "Since it's for a good cause."

She did kiss him then, long and deep, dancing her tongue over his, feeling his heart pick up its beat and race with hers. Then, slowly, she inched away.

"Maybe I wouldn't kiss you like that after five years," she mused.

"Oh, yes, you will." He took her arm and steered her into his cousin's shop.

"Well, well…" Morgana set down a malachite egg she'd been polishing. She'd had an excellent view of the show through her display window. "Another few minutes of that and you'd have stopped traffic."

"An experiment," Sebastian told her. "Morgana knows about the case." Even as Mel's brows drew together, he was continuing. "I don't keep secrets from my family."

"There's no need to worry." Morgana touched Sebastian's arm, but her eyes were on Mel. "We don't keep secrets from each other, but we've had plenty of experience in being…discrete with outsiders."

"I'm sorry. I'm not used to taking people into my confidence."

"It's a risky business," Morgana agreed. "Sebastian, Nash is in the back, grumbling about unloading a shipment. Run along and keep him company for a minute, will you?"

"If you like."

As Sebastian went into the back room, Morgana moved to the door and turned the Closed sign over. She wanted a moment of privacy. "Nash has gotten very protective," she said, turning back. "He worries about me handling boxes and lifting inventory."

"I guess that's natural. In your condition."

"I'm strong as an ox." She smiled and shrugged. "Besides, there are other ways of maneuvering heavy merchandise."

"Hmm" was all Mel could think of to say.

"We don't make a habit of flaunting what we are. Sebastian uses his gift publicly, but people think of it as something one might read about in a supermarket tabloid. They don't really understand what he is or what he has. As for me, the whispers and rumors are good business. And Ana...Ana has her own way of dealing with her talents."

"I really don't know what I'm supposed to say." Mel lifted her hands, then dropped them again. "I don't know if I'll ever take all this in. I never even bought into the tooth fairy."

"That's a pity. Then again, it seems to me that a

very practical mind would be unable to deny what it sees. What it knows."

"I can't deny that he's different. That he has abilities…gifts. And that…" Frustrated, she let her words trail off again. "I've never met anyone like him before."

Morgana gave a low laugh. "Even among the different, Sebastian is unique. One day, perhaps, we'll have time for me to tell you stories. He was always competitive. It continues to infuriate him that he can't cast a decent spell with any real finesse."

Fascinated, Mel stepped closer. "Really?"

"Oh, yes. Of course, I don't tell him just how frustrating it is for me to have to go through all manner of stages to get even a glimpse of the things he can see simply by looking." She waved it away. "But those are old family rivalries. I wanted a moment with you because I realize that Sebastian trusts you enough, obviously cares for you enough, to have opened that part of his life to you."

"I…" Mel blew out a breath. What next? "We're working together," she said carefully. "And you could say that we have a kind of relationship. A personal relationship."

"I'm not going to intrude—overmuch—in that personal relationship. But he is family, and I love him very much. So I have to tell you—don't use this power you have to hurt him."

Mel was flabbergasted. "But you're the witch," she blurted out. Then she blinked. "What I mean is—"

"You said what you meant, aptly. Yes, I am a witch. But I'm also a woman. Who understands power better?"

Mel shook her head. "I don't know what you mean. And I certainly don't know how you think I could possibly hurt Sebastian. If you think I've put him in any danger by involving him in this case—"

"No." Eyes thoughtful, Morgana lifted a hand. "You really don't understand." Morgana's lips curved as her eyes cleared. It was obvious, beautifully obvious, that Mel hadn't a clue that Sebastian was in love with her. "How fascinating," she murmured. "And how delightful."

"Morgana, if you'd just make yourself clear…"

"Oh no, I'd hate to do that." She took both of Mel's hands. "Forgive me for confusing you. We Donovans tend to be protective of each other. I like you," she said with a charming smile. "Very much. I hope we'll be good friends." She gave Mel's hands a squeeze. "I'd like to give you something."

"It isn't necessary."

"Of course not," Morgana agreed, moving toward a display case. "But when I chose this stone, I knew that I would want it to belong to just the right person. Here." She took a slender blue wand attached to a thin silver chain out of the case.

"I can't take that. It must be valuable."

"Value's relative. You don't wear jewelry." Morgana slipped the chain over Mel's head. "But think of this as a talisman. Or a tool, if you like."

Though she'd never been particularly attracted to the things people hung from their ears or crowded on their fingers, she lifted the blue stone to eye level. It wasn't clear, but she could see hints of light through it. In length it was no longer than her thumbnail, but the hues in the stone ranged from pale blue to indigo. "What is it?"

"It's a blue tourmaline. It's an excellent aid for stress." And it was also an excellent channel for joining love with wisdom. But Morgana said nothing of that. "I imagine you have plenty of that in your work."

"My share, I guess. Thanks. It's nice."

"Morgana." Nash poked his head out of the storeroom door. "Oh, hi, Mel."

"Hello."

"Babe, there's this nut on the phone who wants

to know something about green dioptaste on the fourth chakra."

"Customer," Morgana corrected wearily. "It's a customer, Nash."

"Yeah, right. Well this customer wants to expand his heart center." Nash winked at Mel. "Sounds pretty desperate to me."

"I'll take it." She gestured for Mel to follow.

"Know anything about chakras?" Nash murmured to Mel as she walked through the doorway.

"Do you eat it or dance to it?"

He grinned and patted her on the back. "I like you."

"There seems to be a lot of that going around."

Morgana walked into a room beyond. Mel studied the kitchenette, where Sebastian had made himself at home at a wooden table with a beer.

"Want one?"

"You bet." There was the smell of herbs again, from little pots growing on the windowsill. Morgana's voice rose and fell from the next room. "It's an interesting shop."

Sebastian handed her a bottle. "I see you picked up a trinket already."

"Oh." She fingered the stone. "Morgana gave it to me. It's pretty, isn't it?"

"Very."

"So." She turned to Nash. "I really didn't get a chance to tell you before. I love your movies. Especially *Shape Shifter*. It blew me away."

"Yeah?" He was rooting around in the cupboards for cookies. "It has a special place in my heart. Nothing like a sexy lycanthrope with a conscience."

"I like the way you make the illogical logical." She took a sip of beer. "I mean, you make the rules—they might be really weird rules—but then you follow them."

"Mel's big on rules," Sebastian put in.

"Sorry." Morgana stepped back in. "A slight emergency. Nash, you ate all the cookies already."

"All?" Disappointed, he closed the cupboard door.

"Every crumb." She turned to Sebastian. "I imagine you're wondering if the package came in."

"Yes."

She reached into her pocket and took out a small box of hammered silver. "I think you'll find it quite suitable."

He rose to take it from her. Their eyes met, held. "I trust your judgment."

"And I yours." She took his face in her hands and kissed him. "Blessed be, cousin." In a brisk change of mood, she reached for Nash. "Darling, come out in the shop with me. I want to move some things."

"But Mel was just feeding my ego."

"Heavy things," she said, and gave his hand a tug. "We'll see you soon I hope, Mel."

"Yes. Thanks again." The moment the door closed behind them, she looked at Sebastian. "What was that all about?"

"Morgana understood that I preferred to do this alone." He rubbed his thumb over the box as he watched her.

Mel's smile went a little nervous around the edges. "It's not going to hurt, is it?"

"Painless," he promised. At least for her. He opened the box, and offered it.

She peeked in, and would have taken a quick step away if she hadn't been standing with her back to the counter. Inside the ornate little box was a ring. Like the necklace Morgana had given her, it was silver, thin glistening wires woven into an intricate pattern around a center stone of delicate pink with a green rind rim.

"What is it?"

"It's also tourmaline," he told her. "What's called watermelon tourmaline, because of its colors." He took it out. Held it to the light. "Some say it can transfer energy between two people who are important to each other. On a practical level, which I'm sure will interest you, they're used in industry for electri-

cal tuning circuits. They don't shatter at high fre-
quencies like other crystals."

"That's interesting." Her throat was very dry. "But
what's it for?"

Though it was not quite the way he might have
liked it, it would have to do for now. "A wedding
ring," he said, and put it into her hand.

"Excuse me?"

"We would hardly have been married five years
without you having a ring."

"Oh." Surely she was just imagining that the ring
was vibrating in her palm. "That makes sense. Sure.
But why not a plain gold band?"

"Because I prefer this." With his first show of im-
patience, he plucked the ring out of her hand and
shoved it on her finger.

"Okay, okay, don't get testy. It just seems like a
lot of trouble when we could have gone by any department store and picked up—"

"Shut up."

She'd been busy playing with the ring as she
spoke, but now she looked up, narrow-eyed. "Look,
Donovan—"

"For once." He lifted her to her toes. "For once,
do something my way without arguing, without questioning, without making me want to strangle you."

Her eyes heated. "I was stating my opinion. And if this is going to work, we'd better get one thing clear right now. There's no your way, there's no my way. There can only be our way."

Since no amount of searching helped him come up with an argument, he released her. "I have a remarkably even temper," he said, half to himself. "It very rarely flares, because power and temper are a dangerous mix."

Pouting a bit, she rubbed her arms where his fingers had dug in. "Yeah. Right."

"There's one rule, one unbreakable rule, that we live by in my world, Sutherland. 'An it harm none.' I take that very seriously. And for the first time in my life I've come across someone who tempts me to whip up a spell that would have her suffering from all manner of unpleasant discomforts."

She sniffed and picked up her beer again. "You're all wind, Donovan. Your cousin told me you're lousy at spells."

"Oh, there are one or two I've had some luck with." He waited until she'd taken a good swallow of beer, then concentrated. Hard.

Mel choked, gasped and grabbed for her throat. It felt as though she'd just swallowed a slug of pure Kentucky moonshine.

"Particularly spells that involve the mind," Sebastian said smugly while she fought for breath.

"Cute. Real cute." Though the burning had faded, she set the beer aside. There was no point in taking chances. "I don't know what you're all bent out of shape about, Donovan. And I'd really appreciate it if you'd hold the tricks for Halloween, or April Fools' Day, or whenever you all break out for a few laughs."

"Laughs?" He said it much too quietly, taking a step forward. Mel took one to meet him, but whatever they might have done was postponed as the side door swung open.

"Oh." Anastasia, with her hair blowing into her eyes, held the door open with a hip as she balanced a tray of dried flowers. "Excuse me." She didn't need to go any closer to feel the tempers rattling like sabers in the air. "I'll come back later."

"Don't be silly." Sebastian nudged Mel aside— none too gently—and took the tray from his cousin. "Morgana's in the shop."

Hastily, Ana brushed her wayward hair away from her face. "I'll just go tell her I'm here. Nice to see you again, Mel." Ingrained manners had her offering a smile. Then her gaze fixed on the ring. "Oh. How beautiful. It looks like…" She hesitated, flicking a glance at Sebastian. "It looks like it was made for you."

"I'm just kind of borrowing it for a few weeks."

Ana looked at Mel again, and her eyes were kind. "I see. I doubt if I could bear to give something that wonderful back. May I?" Gently Ana took Mel's fingertips and lifted her hand. She recognized the stone as one Sebastian had owned and treasured most of his life. "Yes," she said. "It looks perfect on you."

"Thanks."

"Well, I only have a few minutes, so I'd better let you finish your argument." She tossed Sebastian a quick smile and went out into the shop.

Mel sat on the edge of the table and tilted her head. "Wanna fight?"

He picked up her half-finished beer. "There doesn't seem to be much point in it."

"No, there's not. Because I'm not mad at you. I'm nervous. I've never done anything this big before. Not that I'm afraid I can't handle it."

He sat on the table beside her. "Then what?"

"I guess it's the most important thing I've ever done, and I really…I really care about making it work. Then there's this other thing."

"What other thing?"

"This you-and-me thing. It's important, too."

He took her hand in his. "Yes, it is."

"And I don't want the lines between these two important things to be blurred or mixed up, because I really care about... I really care," she finished.

He brought her fingers to his lips. "So do I."

Sensing that the mood was friendly again, she smiled. "You know what I like about you, Donovan?"

"What?"

"You can do stuff like that—kissing-my-hand stuff. And not look goofy doing it."

"You humble me, Sutherland," he said in a strained voice. "You positively humble me."

Hours later, when the night was quiet and the moonlight dim, she turned to him in sleep. And in sleep her arms slid around him, her body curved to his. He brushed the hair back from her temples as she nestled her head on his shoulder. He rubbed his thumb over the stone on her finger. If he left it there, let his mind drift, he could join her in whatever dream her heart was weaving. It was tempting, almost as tempting as waking her.

Before he could decide which to choose, he had a flash of the stables, the smell of hay and sweat and the distressed whicker of the mare.

Mel blinked awake as she felt him pull away. "What? What?"

"Go back to sleep," he ordered, reaching for a shirt.

"Where are you going?"

"Psyche's ready to foal. I'm going to the stables."

"Oh." Without thinking, she climbed out to search for her clothes. "I'll go with you. Should we call the vet?"

"Ana will come."

"Oh." She fumbled with her buttons in the dark. "Should I call her?"

"Ana will come," he said again, and left her to finish dressing.

Mel hurried after him, pulling on boots on the run. "Should I, like, boil water or something?"

Halfway down the stairs, he stopped and kissed her. "For coffee. Thanks."

"They always boil water," she mumbled, trudging into the kitchen. By the time the coffee was scenting the room, she heard the sound of a car. "Three cups," Mel decided, figuring it was useless to question how Anastasia had known to come.

She found both cousins in the stables. Ana was kneeling beside the mare, murmuring. Beside her were two leather pouches and a rolled cloth.

"She's all right, isn't she?" Mel asked. "I mean, she's healthy?"

"Yes." Ana stroked Psyche's neck. "She's fine. Just fine." Her voice was as soothing as a cool breeze in the desert. The mare responded to it with a quiet whinny. "It won't take long. Relax, Sebastian. It's not the first foal to be born in the world."

"It's her first," he shot back, feeling foolish. He knew it would be all right. He could have told them what sex the foal would be. But that didn't make it any easier to wait while his beloved Psyche suffered through the pangs.

Mel offered him a mug. "Have some coffee, Papa. You could always go pace in the next stall with Eros."

"You might keep him calm, Sebastian," Ana tossed over her shoulder. "It'll help."

"All right."

"Coffee?" Mel eased into the stall to offer Ana a mug.

"Yes, a little." She sat back on her heels to sip.

"Sorry," Mel said when she saw Ana's eyes go wide. "I tend to make it strong."

"It's all right. It'll last me for the next couple of weeks." She opened a pouch and shook some dried leaves and petals into her hand.

"What's that?"

"Just some herbs," Ana said as she fed them to the mare. "To help her with the contractions." She chose three crystals from the other pouch and placed them on the mare's quivering side. She was murmuring now in Gaelic.

The crystals should slide off, Mel thought, staring at them. It was gravity, basic physics. But they remained steady, even as the laboring horse shuddered.

"You have good hands," Ana said. "Stroke her head."

Mel complied. "I really don't know anything about birthing. Well, I had to learn the basics when I was a cop, but I never... Maybe I should..."

"Just stroke her head," Ana repeated gently. "The rest is the most natural thing in the world."

Perhaps it was natural, Mel thought later as she, Sebastian, Ana and the mare labored to bring the foal into the world. But it was also miraculous. She was slick with sweat, her own and the horse's, wired from coffee, and giddy with the idea of helping life into the light.

A dozen times throughout the hours they worked she saw the changes in Ana's eyes. From cool calm gray to smoky concern. From warm amusement to such deep, depthless compassion that Mel's own eyes stung in response.

Once she'd been sure she saw pain in them, a wild, terrified pain that faded only after Sebastian spoke sharply to his cousin.

"Only to give her a moment's relief," she'd said, and Sebastian had shaken his head.

After that it had happened quickly, and Mel had scrambled to help.

"Oh, wow" was the best she could do as she stared at the mare going about the business of cleaning her new son. "I can't believe it. There he is. Just like that."

"It's always a fresh amazement." Ana picked up her pouches and her medical instruments. "Psyche's fine," she continued as she rolled the instruments in the apron she'd put on before the birthing. "The colt, too. I'll come back around this evening for another look, but I'd say mother and son are perfect."

"Thank you, Ana." Sebastian pulled her against him for a hug.

"My pleasure. You did very well for your first foaling, Mel."

"It was incredible."

"Well, I'm going to get cleaned up and head home. I think I'll sleep till noon." Ana kissed Sebastian's cheek, and then, just as casually, kissed Mel's. "Congratulations."

"What a way to spend the night," Mel murmured, and leaned her head against Sebastian's shoulder.

"I'm glad you were here."

"So am I. I never saw anything born before. It makes you realize just how fantastic the whole business is." She yawned hugely. "And exhausting. I wish I could sleep till noon."

"Why don't you?" He tilted his head to kiss her. "Why don't we?"

"I have a business to run. And, since I'm going to be away from it for a couple of weeks, I have a lot of loose ends to tie up."

"You have one to tie up here."

"I do?"

"Absolutely." He swung her up, stained shirt, grubby hands and all. "A few hours ago I was lying in bed thinking about sneaking into one of your dreams with you, or just waking you up."

"Sneaking into one of my dreams?" She gave him a hand by pushing open the door. "Can you do that?"

"Oh, Sutherland, have some faith. In any case," he continued, carrying her straight through the kitchen and into the hall. "Before I did either, we were distracted. So, before you go in to work to tie up loose ends, we'll tie some of our own right here."

"Interesting thought. You may not have noticed, however, that we're both a mess."

"I've noticed." He marched through the master bedroom into the bath. "We're going to have a shower."

"Good idea. I think— Sebastian!"

She shrieked with laughter as he stepped into the shower stall, fully dressed, and turned on the water.

"Idiot. I still have my boots on."

He grinned. "Not for long."

## Chapter 10

Mel wasn't sure how she felt about being Mrs. Donovan Ryan. It certainly seemed to her that Mary Ellen Ryan—her cover persona—was a singularly boring individual, more interested in fashion and manicures than in anything of real importance.

She had to agree it was a good setup. Damn good, she mused as she stepped out onto the deck of the house and studied the glimmer of Lake Tahoe under the moonlight.

The house itself was nothing to sneeze at. Two sprawling levels of contemporary comfort, it was tastefully furnished, decorated with bold colors to reflect the style of its owners.

Mary Ellen and Donovan Ryan, formerly of Seattle, were a modern couple who knew what they wanted.

What they wanted most, of course, was a child.

She'd been impressed with the house when they'd arrived the day before. Impressed enough to comment on the fact that she hadn't expected the FBI to be able to provide such cozy digs so quickly. It was then that Sebastian had casually mentioned that it was one of his properties—something he'd had a whim to pick up about six months before.

Coincidence or witchcraft? Mel thought with a grimace. You be the judge.

"Ready for a night on the town, sweetheart?"

Her grimace turned into a scowl as she turned to Sebastian. "You're not going to start calling me all those dopey names just because we're supposed to be married."

"Heaven forbid." He stepped out on the deck, looking—Mel was forced to admit—about as gorgeous as a man could get in his black dinner suit. "Let's have a look at you."

"I put it all on," she said, struggling not to grumble. "Right down to the underwear you set out."

"You're such a good sport." The sarcasm was light and friendly, and made her lips twitch into a reluctant smile. Taking her hand, he turned her in a circle. Yes, he thought, the red evening pants had been an excellent choice. The fitted silver jacket went quite well with them, as did the ruby drops at her ears. "You look wonderful. Try to act like you believe it."

"I hate wearing heels. And do you know what they did to my hair?"

His lips curved as he flicked a finger over it. It was sleeked back in a sassy, side-parted bob. "Very chic."

"Easy for you to say. You didn't have some maniacal woman with a French accent glopping up your head with God knows what, spraying stuff on it, snipping and crimping and whatnot until you wanted to scream."

"Hard day, huh?"

"That's not the half of it. I had to get my nails done. You have no idea what that's like. They come at you with these little scissors and probes and files and smelly bottles, and they talk to you about their boyfriends and ask personal questions about your sex life. And you have to act like you're just enjoying the hell out of it. I almost had to have a facial." She shuddered with complete sincerity. "I don't know what they'd have done to me, but I said I had to get home and fix dinner."

"A narrow escape."

"If I really had to go to a beauty parlor once a week for the rest of my life, I think I'd slit my throat."

"Buck up, Sutherland."

"Right." She sighed, feeling better. "Well, it wasn't hard to start spreading it around how I had this wonderful husband and this great new house and how we'd been trying for years to have a baby. They just lap that kind of stuff up. I went on about how we'd had all these tests and had been trying these fertility drugs, and how long the lists were at adoption agencies. They were very sympathetic."

"Good job."

"Better, I got the name of two lawyers and a doctor. The doctor's supposed to be some miracle gynecologist. One of the lawyers was the manicurist's cousin, and the other was supposed to have helped the sister-in-law of this lady getting a permanent to adopt two Romanian babies last year."

"I believe I follow that," Sebastian said after a moment.

"I figured we should check it out. Tomorrow I'm going to the health club. While they're pummeling me, I can go through the routine."

"There's no law that says you can't enjoy a sauna and massage while you're at it."

She hesitated, and was grateful that the roomy pockets of the evening pants made a home for her hands. "It makes me feel... I know you're putting a lot of your money into this."

"I have plenty." He tipped a finger under her chin. "If I didn't want to use it this way, I wouldn't. I remember how Rose looked when you brought her to me, Mel. And I remember Mrs. Frost. We're in this together."

"I know." She curled her fingers around his wrist. "I should be thanking you instead of complaining."

"But you complain so well." When she grinned, he kissed her. "Come on, Sutherland. Let's gamble. I'm feeling lucky."

The Silver Palace was one of Tahoe's newest and most opulent hotel casinos. White swans glided in the silvery waters of the lobby pool, and man-sized urns exploded with exotic flowers. The staff was dressed in spiffy tuxedos with trademark silver ties and cummerbunds.

They passed a number of elegant shops displaying everything from diamonds and furs to T-shirts. Mel figured they'd aligned them close enough to the casino to tempt any winners to put their money back into the hotel.

The casino itself was crowded with sound, the chink-chink of coins pouring out of slots echoing from the high ceilings. There was the hubbub of voices, the clatter of the roulette wheels, the smell of smoke and liquor and perfumes. And, of course, of money.

"Some joint," Mel commented, taking a gander at the knights and fair ladies painted on the windowless walls.

"What's your game?"

She shrugged. "They're all sucker's games. Trying to win against the house is like trying to row upstream with one oar. You might make some progress, but the current's going to carry you down sooner or later."

He nipped lightly at her ear. "You're not here to be practical. We're on our second honeymoon, remember? Sweetie pie?"

"Yuck," she said distinctly through a bright, loving smile. "Okay, let's buy some chips."

She opted to start off with the slots, deciding they were mindless enough to allow her to play while still absorbing her surroundings. They were there to make contact with Jasper Gumm, the man who'd held Parkland's IOU. Mel was well aware it could take several nights to reach that next step.

She lost steadily, then won back a few dollars, automatically feeding the coins back into the machine. She found there was something oddly appealing about the whoosh and jingle, the occasional squeal from another player, the bells and lights that rang and flashed when someone hit the jackpot.

It was relaxing, she realized, and tossed a smile over her shoulder to Sebastian. "I don't guess the house has to worry about me breaking the bank."

"Perhaps if you went at it less…aggressively." He put a hand over hers as she pulled the lever. Lights whirled. Bells clanged.

"Oh!" Her eyes went huge as coins began to shoot into the basket. "Oh, wow! That's five hundred!" She did a little dance, then threw her arms around him. "I won five hundred dollars." She gave him a big, smacking kiss, then froze with her mouth an inch from his. "Oh, God, Donovan, you cheated."

"What a thing to say. Outwitting a machine isn't cheating." He could see her sense of fair play warring with her elation. "Come on, you can lose it back at blackjack."

"I guess it's okay. It's for a higher cause."

"Absolutely."

Laughing, she began to scoop the coins into the bucket beside the machine. "I like to win."

"So do I."

They scoped out the tables, sipping champagne and playing the part of an affectionate couple on a night out. She tried not to take it too seriously, the attention he paid her, the fact that his hand was always there when she reached for it.

They were lovers, yes, but they weren't in love. They cared for and respected each other—but that was a long way from happily-ever-after. The ring on her finger was only a prop, the house they shared only a cover.

One day she would have to give the ring back and move out of the house. They might continue to see each other, at least for a time. Until his work and hers took them in different directions.

People didn't last in her life. She'd come to accept that. Or always had before. Now, when she thought of heading off in that different direction alone, without him, there was an emptiness inside her that was almost unbearable.

"What is it?" Instinctively he put a hand at the base of her neck to rub. "You're tensing up."

"Nothing. Nothing." Even with the rule about him not looking into her mind, he was much too perceptive. "I guess I'm impatient to move. Let's try this table. See what happens."

He didn't press, though he was quite certain that something more than the case was troubling her. When they took their seats at a five-dollar table, he slipped an arm around her shoulders so that they played the cards together.

She played well, he noted, her practical nature and quick wits keeping her even with the house for the first hour. He could see by the casual way she scanned the room that she was taking everything in. The security guards, the cameras, the two-way glass on the second level.

Sebastian ordered more champagne and began to do his own probing.

The man next to him was sweating over a seventeen and worrying that his wife suspected he was having an affair. His wife sat next to him, chain-smoking and trying to imagine how the dealer would look naked.

Sebastian fastidiously left her to it.

Next to Mel was a cowboy type tossing back bourbon and branch water while he won at a slow but steady pace. His mind was a jumble of thoughts about treasury bonds, livestock and the spread of cards. He was also wishing that the little filly beside him had come to the table alone.

Sebastian smiled to himself, wondering how Mel would feel about being called a little filly.

As he mentally roamed the table, Sebastian got impressions of boredom, excitement, desperation and greed. He found what he wanted in the young couple directly across from him.

They were from Columbus, on the third night of their honeymoon. They were barely old enough to be at the tables, they were deliriously in love, and they had decided, after much calculation, that the excitement of gambling was worth the hundred-dollar stake.

They were down to fifty now, and they were having the time of their lives.

Sebastian saw the husband—Jerry was his name—hesitating over hitting fifteen. He gave him a little push. Jerry signaled for another card and went pop-eyed when he pulled a six.

With a subtle and enjoyable magic, Sebastian had young Jerry doubling his stake, then tripling it, while the young couple gasped and giggled over their astonishing luck.

"They're sure raking it in," Mel commented.

"Mmm." Sebastian sipped his wine.

Oblivious to the gentle persuasion, Jerry began to up his bets. Word spread, as it does in such places, that there was a winner at table three. People began to mill around, applauding and slapping the baffled Jerry on the shoulder as his winnings piled up.

"Oh, Jerry!" His new wife, Karen, clung to him.

"Maybe we should stop. It's almost enough for a down payment on a house. Maybe we should just stop."

Sorry, Sebastian thought, and gave her a little mental nudge.

Karen bit her lip. "No. Keep going." She buried her face against his shoulder and laughed. "It's like magic."

The comment had Mel looking up from her own cards and sending Sebastian a narrow-eyed look. "Donovan."

"Shh." He patted her hand. "I have my reasons."

Mel began to understand them as the nearly delirious Jerry hovered at the ten-thousand dollar mark. A husky man in a tuxedo approached the table. He had a dignified bearing to go with smoothly tanned skin, a sun-tipped mustache and expertly styled hair. Mel was certain he was the kind of man most women would look at more than twice.

But she took an instant dislike to his eyes. They were pale blue, and, though they were smiling, she felt a quick chill race up her spine.

"Bad business," she muttered, and felt Sebastian's hand close over hers.

The crowd that had gathered cheered again as the dealer lost to Jerry on nineteen.

"This seems to be your lucky night."

"Boy, I'll say." Jerry looked up at the newcomer with

dazed eyes. "I've never won anything before in my life."

"Are you staying at the hotel?"

"Yeah. Me and my wife." He gave Karen a squeeze. "This is the first night we tried the tables."

"Then allow me to congratulate you personally. I'm Jasper Gumm. This is my hotel."

Mel slanted Sebastian a look. "Pretty sneaky way to get a look at him."

"A roundabout route," he agreed. "But an enjoyable one."

"Hmm… Have your young hero and heroine finished for the evening?"

"Oh, yes, they're quite finished."

"Excuse me a minute." Taking her glass, Mel got up to stroll around the table. Sebastian had been right. The young couple were already making noises about cashing in and were busily thanking Gumm.

"Be sure to come back," Gumm told them. "We like to think that everyone at the Silver Palace walks away a winner."

When Gumm turned, Mel made certain she was directly in his path. A quick movement, and her champagne splattered.

"Oh, I beg your pardon." She brushed at his damp sleeve. "How clumsy of me."

"Not at all. It was my fault." Easing away from the dispersing crowd, he took out a handkerchief to dry her hand. "I'm afraid I was distracted." He glanced at her empty glass. "And I owe you a drink."

"No, that's kind of you, but it was nearly empty." She flashed him a smile. "Fortunately for your suit. I suppose I was a little curious about all those chips. My husband and I were across the table from that young couple. And not having nearly their luck."

"Then I definitely owe you a drink." Gumm took her arm just as Sebastian walked up.

"Darling, you're supposed to drink the champagne, not pour it on people."

As if she were flustered, she laughed and ran a hand down his arm. "I've already apologized."

"No harm done," Gumm assured them as he offered Sebastian a hand. "Jasper Gumm."

"Donovan Ryan. My wife, Mary Ellen."

"A pleasure. Are you guests of the hotel?"

"No, actually, we've just moved to Tahoe." Sebastian sent an affectionate glance to Mel. "We're taking a few days as a kind of second honeymoon before we get back to business."

"Welcome to the community. Now I definitely must replace that champagne." He signalled to a roving waitress.

"It's very kind of you." Mel glanced around approvingly. "You have a wonderful place here."

"Now that we're neighbors, I hope you'll enjoy the facilities. We have an excellent dining room." As he spoke, Gumm took stock. The woman's jewelry was discreet and expensive. The man's dinner suit was expertly tailored. Both of them showed the panache of quiet affluence. Just the type of clientele he preferred.

When the waitress returned with a fresh bottle and glasses, Gumm poured the wine himself. "What business are you in, Mr. Donovan?"

"Real estate. Mary Ellen and I spent the last few years in Seattle, and we decided it was time for a change. My business allows me to be flexible."

"And yours?" Gumm asked Mel.

"I've put my career on hold, at least for a while. I thought I'd like keeping a home."

"Ah, and children."

"No." Her smile wobbled as she looked down at her glass. "No, not yet. But I think the weather here, the sun, the lake…would be a wonderful place to raise a family." There was a trace, just a hint, of desperation in her voice.

"I'm sure. Please enjoy the Silver Palace. Don't be strangers."

"Oh, I'm sure we'll be back," Sebastian assured

him. "Nicely done," he murmured to Mel when they were alone.

"I thought so. Do you think we should go back to the tables for a while or just wander about looking moon-eyed at each other?"

He chuckled, started to pull her close for a kiss, then stopped, his hand on her shoulder. "Well, well… sometimes things just fall neatly into place."

"What?"

"Drink your champagne, my love, and smile." He turned her gently, keeping his arm around her as they wandered toward the roulette table. "Now look over there, to the woman Gumm is speaking with. The redhead by the staircase."

"I see her." Mel leaned her head against Sebastian's shoulder. "Five-five, a hundred and ten, light complexion. Twenty-eight, maybe thirty years old."

"Her name's Linda—or it is now. It was Susan when she checked into the motel with David."

"She's—" Mel nearly took a step forward before she stopped herself. "What's she doing here?"

"Sleeping with Gumm, I imagine. Waiting for the next job."

"We have to find out how much they know. How close they are to the top." Grimly she finished off the champagne. "You work your way, I'll work mine."

"Agreed."

When Mel saw that Linda was heading for the ladies' lounge, she shoved her empty glass into Sebastian's hand. "Hold this."

"Of course, darling," he murmured to her retreating back.

Mel bided her time, sitting at one of the curvy dressing tables, freshening her lipstick, powdering her nose. When Linda sat at the table next to hers, she began the process all over again.

"Shoot," Mel said in disgust, examining her fingers. "I chipped a nail."

Linda sent her a sympathetic glance. "Don't you hate that?"

"I'll say, especially since I just had them done this morning. I have the worst luck with them." She searched through her bag for the nail file she knew wasn't there. "Your nails are gorgeous."

"Thank you." The redhead held up a hand to examine. "I have a marvelous manicurist."

"Do you?" Mel shifted and crossed her legs. "I wonder... My husband and I just moved here from Seattle. I really need to find the right beautician, health club, that sort of thing."

"You can't do better than right here at the hotel for either. Nonguest membership fees for the health club are a bit pricey, but believe me, it's well worth it." She fluffed at her luxuriant mane. "And the beauty shop is top-notch."

"I appreciate that. I'll look into it."

"Just tell them Linda sent you, Linda Glass."

"I will," Mel said as she rose. "Thanks a lot."

"No problem." Linda slicked on lip gloss. If the woman joined the club, she thought, she'd get a nice commission. Business was business.

A few hours later, Mel was flopped on her stomach in the center of the bed, making a list. She wore a baggy pajama top, her favored lounging choice, and had already disarranged her sleek coiffure into tousled spikes with restless fingers.

She'd be using the Silver Palace's facilities, all right, she thought. Starting tomorrow, she would join their health club, check out their beauty parlor. And, Lord help her, make an appointment for a facial, or whatever other torture they had in mind.

With any luck, she could be cozied up to Linda Glass and exchanging girl talk within twenty-four hours.

"What are you up to, Sutherland?"

"Plan B," she said absently. "I like to have a plan B in reserve in case plan A bombs. Do you think leg waxing hurts?"

"I wouldn't hazard a guess." He ran a fingertip down her calf. "However, yours feel smooth enough to me."

"Well, I have to be prepared to spend half my day in this place, so I have to have something for them to do to me." She cocked her head to look up at him. He was standing beside the bed, wearing the bottoms of the baggy pajamas and swirling a brandy.

I guess we look like a unit, she thought. Like an actual couple having a little chat before bedtime.

The idea had her doodling on the pad. "Do you really like that stuff?"

"Which stuff?"

"That brandy. It always tastes like medicine to me."

"Perhaps you've never had the right kind." He handed her the snifter. Mel braced up on her elbows to sample it while he straddled her and sat back on his heels. "You're still tense," he commented, and began to rub her shoulders.

"A little wired, maybe. I guess I'm starting to think this really may work—the job, I mean."

"It's going to work. While you're having your incredibly long and lovely legs waxed, I'm going to be playing golf—at the same club Gumm belongs to."

Far from convinced the brandy had anything going for it, she looked back over her shoulder. "Then we'll see who finds out more, won't we?"

"We will indeed."

"There's this spot on my shoulder blade." She arched like a cat. "Yeah, that's it. I wanted to ask you about that couple tonight. The big winners."

"What about them?" He pushed the shirt up out of his way and pleased himself by exploring the long, narrow span of her back.

"I know it was your way of getting Gumm to the table, but it doesn't seem exactly straight, you know? Making him win ten thousand."

"I merely influenced his decisions. And I imagine Gumm's taken in much more than that by selling children."

"Yeah, yeah, and I can sort of see the justice in that. But that couple—what if they try to do it again and lose their shirts? Maybe they won't be able to stop, and—"

He chuckled, pressing his lips to the center of her back. "I'm more subtle than that. Young Jerry and Karen will put a down payment on a nice house in the suburbs, astonish their friends with their good fortune. They'll both agree that they've used up all of their luck on this one shot, and rarely gamble again. They'll have three children. And they'll have a spot of fairly serious marital trouble in their sixth year, but they'll work it out."

"Well." Mel wondered if she'd ever get used to it. "In that case."

"In that case," he murmured, running his lips down her spine. "Why don't you put it out of your mind and concentrate on me?"

Smiling to herself, she set the brandy on the chest at the foot of the bed. "Maybe I could." She flipped, then twisted, getting a solid grip before shoving him back on the bed. With her hands clamped on his, she leaned down until they were nose-to-nose. "Gotcha."

He grinned, then nipped her lower lip. "Yes, you do."

"And I might just keep you a while." She kissed the tip of his nose, then his cheek, his chin, his lips. "The brandy tastes better on you than it does in the glass."

"Try again, just to be sure."

With humor bright in her eyes, she lowered her mouth to his and sampled long and deep. "Mmm-hmm. A definite improvement. I do like your taste, Donovan." She linked her fingers with his, pleased that he made no move to break the contact when she slid down to nibble at his throat.

She teased him, toying with his desire and her own as she savored his flesh. Warm here, cooler there, the rich beat of a pulse beneath her lips. She enjoyed the shape of his body, the width of his shoulders, the hard, smooth chest, the quick quiver of his flat belly under her touch.

She liked the way her hand looked gliding over him, her skin shades lighter than his, the ring glowing with its meld of colors against the silver. Rubbing her cheek over him, she felt not just passion, but a deep, drugging emotion that welled up like wine and clouded her senses.

Her throat stung with it, her eyes burned, and her heart all but melted out of her chest.

With a sigh, she brought her lips back to his.

It was she who was the witch tonight, he thought, wallowing in her. She who had the power and the gift. She had taken his heart, his soul, his needs, his future, and had them cupped delicately in her hands.

He murmured his love for her, again and again, but the language of his blood was Gaelic, and she didn't understand.

They moved together, flowing over the bed as if it were an enchanted lake. As the moon began to set, shifting night closer to day, they were lost in each other, surrounded by the magic each brought to the other.

When she rose over him, her body glimmering in the lamplight, her eyes dark with desires, heavy with pleasures, he thought she had never looked more beautiful. Or more his.

He reached for her. And she answered. Their bodies blended. The moment was sweet and fine and fierce.

She arched back, taking more of him, shuddering with the glory of it.

Their hands met, and held, gripping firm as they rose toward the next pinnacle.

When they could go no higher, when he had emptied himself into her and their flesh was weak and wet from love, she slid down to him, hardly aware that her eyes were damp. She buried her face at his throat, shivering as his arms came around her.

"Don't let go," she murmured. "All night. Don't let go all night."

"I won't."

He held her while her heart struggled with the knowledge that it loved, and until her body gave way to weariness and slept.

## Chapter 11

It wasn't so difficult to get a look at the appointment books for the beauty shop and health club in the Silver Palace. If you smiled enough and tipped enough, Mel knew, you could get a look at most anything. And by tipping a little more, it was easy to match her schedule with Linda Glass's.

That was the simple part. The hard part for Mel was the prospect of spending an entire day wearing a leotard.

When she took her place in the aerobics class with a dozen other women, she sent a friendly smile in Linda's direction.

"So, you're giving it a try." The redhead checked to see that her mane was still bundled attractively in its band.

"I really appreciate the tip," Mel responded. "With the move, I've missed over a week. It doesn't take long to get out of shape."

"Don't I know it. Whenever I travel—" She broke off when the instructor switched on a recorder. Out poured a catchy rock ballad.

"Time to stretch, ladies." All smiles and firm muscles, the instructor turned to face the mirror at the head of the class. "Now, reach!" she said in her perky voice as she demonstrated.

Mel followed along through the stretches and the warm-up and into the more demanding routines. Though she considered herself in excellent shape, she had to give all her attention to the moves. Obviously she'd plopped herself down in a very advanced class, and there was a matter of grace and style, as well as endurance.

Before the class was half-over, she developed a deep loathing for the bouncy instructor, with her pert ponytail and cheerful voice.

"One more leg lift, and I'm jumping her," Mel muttered. Although she hadn't meant to speak aloud, it was apparently the perfect move. Linda flashed her a grim smile.

"I'm right behind you." She panted as she executed what the instructor gleefully called hitch kicks. "She can't be over twenty. She deserves to die."

Mel chuckled and puffed. When the music stopped, the women sagged together in a sweaty heap.

After pulse checks and cool-downs, Mel dropped down next to Linda and buried her face in a towel. "That's what I get for taking ten days off." With a weary sigh, Mel lowered the towel. "I can't believe I scheduled myself for an entire day."

"I know what you mean. I've got weight training next."

"Really?" Mel offered her a surprised smile. "So do I."

"No kidding?" Linda blotted her neck, then rose. "I guess we might as well go suffer through it together."

They moved from weights to stationary bikes, from bikes to treadmills. The more they sweated, the friendlier they became. Conversation roamed from exercise to men, from men to backgrounds.

They shared a sauna and a whirlpool, and ended the session with a massage.

"I can't believe you gave up your career to keep a house." Stretched on the padded table, Linda folded her arms under her chin. "I can't imagine it."

"I'm not used to it myself." Mel sighed as the

masseuse worked her way down her spine. "To tell you the truth, I haven't quite figured out what to do with myself yet. But it's a kind of experiment."

"Oh?"

She hesitated, just enough to let Linda know it was a sensitive subject. "You see, my husband and I have been trying to start a family. No luck. Since we've gone through the whole route of tests and procedures without results, I had this idea that if I quit for a while, maybe shucked off some of the career tension…well, something might happen."

"It must be difficult."

"It is. We both—I suppose since we're only children ourselves and don't have anyone but each other, we really want a large family. It seems so unjust, really. Here we have this wonderful house, we're solid financially, and our marriage is good. But we just can't seem to have children."

If the wheels were clicking in Linda's head, she masked it with sympathy. "I guess you've been trying for a while now."

"Years. It's really my fault. The doctors have told us there's a very slim chance that I'd be able to conceive."

"I don't mean to offend you, but have you ever thought of adoption?"

"Thought about it?" Mel managed a sad smile. "I

can't tell you how many lists we're on. Both of us agree that we could love a child that wasn't biologically ours. We feel we have so much to give, but..." She sighed again. "I suppose it's selfish, but we really want a baby. It might be a little easier to adopt an older child, but we're holding out. We've been told it could take years. I don't know how we'll handle all those empty rooms." She made her eyes fill, then blinked away the tears. "I'm sorry. I shouldn't go on about it. I get maudlin."

"That's all right." Linda stretched her arm between the tables to squeeze Mel's hand. "I guess no one can really understand like another woman."

They shared an iced juice and a spinach salad for lunch. Mel allowed Linda to guide the conversation gently back to her personal life. As the naive and deeply emotional Mary Ellen Ryan, she poured out information about her marriage, her hopes, her fears. She sprinkled in a few tears for good measure, and bravely wiped them away.

"You aren't thinking marriage yourself?" Mel asked.

"Me? Oh, no." Linda laughed. "I tried it once, a long time ago. It's too confining for me. Jasper and I have a very nice arrangement. We're fond of each other, but we don't let it interfere with business. I like being able to come and go as I please."

"I admire you." *You coldhearted floozy.* "Before I met Donovan, I had the idea that I'd go it alone through life, carving out my niche. Not that I regret falling in love and getting married, but I guess we all envy the woman who makes her own."

"It suits me. But you're doing all right. You've got a guy who's crazy about you, and he's done well enough that you've got a nice home. Just about perfect."

Mel looked down at her empty glass. "Just about."

"Once you have that baby, it'll be perfect." Linda patted her hand. "Take my word for it."

Mel dragged herself home, tossing her gym bag one way and kicking her shoes the other.

"There you are." Sebastian was looking down from the upstairs balcony. "I was about to send out a search party."

"You'd do better with a stretcher."

His smile faded. "Are you hurt?" He was already starting down the steps. "I knew I should've kept an eye on you."

"Hurt?" She all but growled at him. "You don't know the half of it. I had the aerobics instructor from hell. Her name was Penny, if that gives you a clue. And she was cute as a damn button. Then I got handed over to some Amazon queen named Madge who put me on weights and all these hideous shiny machines. I pumped and lifted and squatted and crunched." Wincing, she pressed a hand to her stomach. "And all I've had to eat all day is a few stingy leaves."

"Aw." He kissed her brow. "Poor baby."

Her eyes narrowed. "I'm in the mood to punch someone, Donovan. It could be you."

"How about if I fix you a nice snack?"

Her lips moved into a pout. "Have we got any frozen pizza?"

"I sincerely doubt it. Come on." He put a friendly arm around her shoulders as he led her into the kitchen. "You can tell me all about it while you eat."

She dropped down agreeably at the smoked glass kitchen table. "It was quite a day. You know she— Linda—does this whole routine twice a week?" Inspired, Mel popped up again to root through the cupboards for a bag of chips. "I don't know why anybody'd want to be that healthy," she said with her mouth full. "She seems okay, really. I mean, when you talk to her, she comes across as a normal, bright lady." Eyes grim, she sat again. "Then you keep talking, and you get to see that she's plenty bright. She's also cold as a fish."

"I take it you talked quite a bit." Sebastian glanced up from his construction of a king-size sandwich.

"Hell, yes. I spilled my guts to her. She knows how I lost my parents when I was twenty. How I met you a couple years later. The whole love-at-first-sight routine. And you were pretty romantic." She crunched into a chip.

"Was I?" He set the sandwich and a glass of her favorite soft drink in front of her.

"You bet. Showered me with roses, took me dancing and for long moonlit walks. You were nuts about me."

He smiled as she bit hungrily into the sandwich. "I'm sure I was."

"You begged me to marry you. Lord, this is good." She closed her eyes and swallowed. "Where was I?"

"I was begging you to marry me."

"Right." She gestured with her glass before drinking. "But I was cautious. I did move in with you eventually, and then I let you wear me down. You've done everything to make my life a fairy tale since."

"I sound like a terrific guy."

"Oh, yeah. I really played that up. We are the world's happiest couple. Except for our one heart-break." She frowned but kept on eating. "You know, in the beginning I was starting to feel pretty bad about stringing her along. I knew it was a job, an important job, but it just seemed so calculating. She was nice, friendly, and I felt uncomfortable the way I was setting her up."

She reached for the chips again, nibbling as she worked through her own thoughts. "Then, once I brought up the baby business, I could practically see her go sharp, you know? All those soft edges just cleaved away. She was still smiling and sympathetic and friendly as hell, but she was clicking it all into that brain of hers and figuring the angles. So I didn't feel bad about letting her pry more information out of me. I want her, Donovan."

"You'll be seeing her again soon?"

"Day after tomorrow. At the beauty parlor, for the works." With a little moan, Mel pushed her plate away. "She thinks I'm a woman trying to fill the time on her hands." She grimaced. "Shopping was mentioned."

"How we suffer for our work."

"Very funny. Since you spent the morning hitting a little white ball around."

"I don't suppose I mentioned that I detest golf."

"No." She grinned. "Good. Tell me how it went."

"We ran into each other on the fourth tee. Quite by accident, of course."

"Of course."

"So we ended up playing the rest of the course

together." Sebastian picked up her half-finished drink and sipped. "He finds my wife quite charming."

"Naturally."

"We discussed business, his and mine. He's interested in making some investments, so I made a few real estate suggestions."

"Clever."

"I do have some property in Oregon I've been thinking about selling. Anyway, we had a drink afterward and discussed sports and other manly things. I managed to drop into the conversation the fact that I hoped to have a son."

"Not just a kid?"

"As I said, it was a manly sort of event. A son to carry on the name, to play ball with, slipped more seamlessly into the conversation."

"Girls play ball," she muttered. "Never mind. Did he pick up on it?"

"Only quite delicately. I fumbled a bit, looked distressed, and changed the subject."

"Why?" She straightened in her chair. "If you had him on the line, why'd you cut him loose?"

"Because it felt right. You'll have to trust me on this, Mel. Gumm would have been suspicious if I'd taken him into my confidence so quickly. With you and the woman it's different. More natural."

She mulled it over, and, though she was still frowning, nodded. "All right. I'm inclined to agree. And we've certainly laid the groundwork."

"I spoke with Devereaux just before you got in. They should have a full work-up on Linda Glass by tomorrow, and he'll let us know as soon as Gumm makes a move to check out our story."

"Good enough."

"Also, we're invited to dine with Gumm and his lady on Friday evening."

Mel cocked a brow. "Even better." She leaned forward to kiss him. "You did good work, Donovan."

"I suppose we make a fair team. Have you finished eating?"

"For now."

"Then I think we should prepare for Friday night."

"Prepare what?" She shot him a suspicious look as he pulled her to her feet. "If you're going to start fiddling around with what I'm supposed to wear…"

"Not at all. It's this way," he told her as they walked out of the kitchen. "We're going to be a devoted and deliriously happy married couple."

"Yeah, so?"

"Madly in love," he continued, drawing her toward the stairs.

"I know the drill, Donovan."

"Well, I firmly believe in the Method school of acting. So I'm quite sure it will help our performance if we spend as much time as possible making love."

"Oh, I see." She turned, twining her arms around his neck and backing into the bedroom. "Well, like you said, we have to suffer for our work."

Mel was certain that one day she would look back and laugh. Or at least she would look back with the grim satisfaction of having survived.

Since going into law enforcement she had been kicked, cursed, slugged and insulted, had doors slammed in her face and on her foot. She'd been threatened, propositioned and, on one memorable occasion, she'd been shot at.

All of that was nothing compared to what was being done to her in the Silver Woman.

The hotel's exclusive and expansive beauty salon offered everything from a wash and set to something exotically—and terrifyingly—termed body wrapping.

Mel hadn't had the courage for that one, but she was getting the treatment from head to toe—and every inch between.

She arrived moments before Linda and, falling back on her established persona, greeted the woman like an old friend.

During leg waxing—which, Mel discovered quickly enough, did hurt—they discussed clothes and hairstyles. Smiling through gritted teeth, Mel was glad she'd boned up for hours the night before with fashion magazines.

Later, while whatever pungent glop the beautician smeared on her face hardened, Mel chatted about how much she was enjoying living in Tahoe.

"Our view of the lake is incredible. I really can't wait until we get to know more people. I love to entertain."

"Jasper and I can introduce you around," Linda offered as the pedicurist buffed her toenails. "Being in the hotel business, we know just about everyone you'd want to know."

"That would be marvellous." Mel chanced a look down and tried to look pleased, rather than horrified, that her toenails were being painted fuchsia. "Donovan mentioned to me that he met Jasper on the golf course at the club. Donovan just loves playing golf," she said, hoping it trapped him into spending hours on the green. "It's more a passion than a hobby."

"Jasper's the same way. I can't work up an interest

in it myself." She began to chat about different people she wanted Mel to meet, and about how they might get together for tennis or sailing.

Mel agreed animatedly, wondering if a person could actually die of boredom.

Her face was scrubbed clean, and cream was slathered on. Some sort of oil was squirted all over her hair, and then plastic was wrapped around it.

"I just love being pampered this way," Linda murmured. They were both lying back in soft chairs, having their hands massaged and their nails done.

"Me too," Mel said, and prayed they were nearly finished.

"I suppose that's why this job suits me. Most of the time I work nights, so my days are free. And I can make use of all the hotel's benefits."

"Have you worked here long?"

"Almost two years now." She sighed. "It's never dull."

"I imagine you meet all sorts of fascinating people."

"The high-powered sort. That's what I like. From what you were saying the other day, your husband doesn't sound like small change."

Mel would have grinned, but she settled for an indulgent smile. "Oh, he does very well. You could say that Donovan has the magic touch."

They were rinsed, their scalps were massaged—
Mel actually found it quite enjoyable—and it was
nearly time for the finishing touches. She realized
that if Linda didn't probe soon she would have to find
an opening to bring up the subject herself.

"You know, Mary Ellen, I was thinking about what
you told me the other day."

"Oh." Mel feigned discomfort. "I'm so sorry
about that, Linda, dumping on you that way, and so
soon after we'd met. I guess I was feeling a little lost
and homesick."

"Nonsense." Linda waved her glorious nails. "I
think we just hit it off, that's all. You were comfortable with me."

"Yes, I was. But I'm more than a little embarrassed to think that I bored you with all that business
about my personal life."

"I wasn't bored at all. I was touched." Her voice
was smooth as silk, with just the right touch of
sympathy. Mel felt her hackles rising. "And it made
me think. Please tell me if I'm getting too personal.
But have you ever considered private adoption?"

"You mean going through a lawyer who works
with unwed mothers?" Mel gave a long, wistful sigh.
"Actually, we did try that route once, about a year
ago. We weren't quite sure it was right. It wasn't that
the money was a problem, but we were concerned

about the legality, and the morality. But it all seemed perfect. We even went so far as to have an interview with the mother. Our hopes were very high. Too high. We picked our names, and window-shopped for baby things. It really looked as if it was going to happen. At the last minute, she backed out."

Mel bit her lower lip, as if to steady herself.

"That must have been dreadful for you."

"We both took it very hard. To get that close and then…nothing. We haven't discussed trying that way again since."

"I can understand that. But, as it happens, I do know of someone who's had a great deal of luck placing babies with adoptive parents."

Mel closed her eyes. She was afraid they would fill with derision, not hope. "A lawyer?"

"Yes. I don't know him personally, but, as I said, you meet a lot of people in this business, and I've heard. I don't want to promise, or get your hopes up, but if you'd like, I could check."

"I'd be very grateful." Mel opened her eyes and met Linda's in the mirror. "I can't tell you how grateful."

An hour later, Mel swung out of the hotel and into Sebastian's arms. She laughed as he dipped her back for an exaggerated kiss.

"What are you doing here?"

"Playing the dutiful, lovesick husband come to fetch his wife." He held her at arm's length and smiled. Her hair was fluffed into a sexy, windblown look, her eyes were deepened and enlarged with blending shadows, and her lips were the same slick fuchsia as her nails. "In the name of Finn, Sutherland, what have they done to you?"

"Don't smirk."

"I'm not. You look extraordinary. Stunning. Just not quite like my Mel." He tipped her chin up for another kiss. "Who is this elegant, polished woman I'm holding?"

Not as annoyed as she wanted to be, she pulled a face. "You'd better not make fun after what I've been through. I actually had a bikini wax. It was barbaric." Chuckling, she linked her hands around his neck. "And my toenails are pink."

"I can't wait to see." He kissed her again, lightly. "I have news."

"Me too."

"Why don't I take a walk with my gorgeous wife and tell her how Gumm's been putting out feelers on the estimable Ryans of Seattle?"

"All right." She linked her fingers with his. "And I'll tell you how, out of the goodness of her heart,

Linda Glass is going to help us make contact with a lawyer. About a private adoption."

"We do work well together."

"Yes, we do, Donovan." Pleased with herself, she strolled beside him. "We certainly do."

From the presidential suite on the top floor of the Silver Palace, Gumm watched through the window. "A charming couple," he commented to Linda.

"They're certainly loopy for each other." She sipped champagne as Sebastian and Mel walked off hand in hand. "The way she looks when she says his name almost makes me wonder if they're really married."

"I've had copies of the marriage certificate and other papers faxed in. It all seems in order." He tapped his fingers to his lips. "If they were a plant, I can't imagine they'd be so easily intimate."

"Plant?" Linda gave him a worried look. "Come on, Jasper, why would you even consider it? There's no way back to us."

"The business with the Frosts concerns me."

"Well, it's too bad they lost the kid. But we got our fee, and we didn't leave a trail."

"We left Parkland. I haven't been able to locate him."

"So he dropped off the edge of the world." Linda

shrugged and moved over to press her body to Gumm's. "You've got nothing to worry about there. You held his note, and it was legit."

"He saw you."

"He wasn't seeing much of anything, as panicked as he was. Plus, it was dark, and I was wearing a scarf. Parkland doesn't worry me." She touched her lips to his. "We've got the touch, babe. Being in an organization like this, we've got so many covers and trapdoors, they'll never come close to us. And the money…" She loosened his tie. "Just think how that money keeps pouring in."

"You do like the money, don't you?" He tugged down the zipper of her dress. "We've got that in common."

"We've got lots in common. This could be a big one for us. We pass the Ryans along, there will be a nice fat commission in it. I guarantee they'll pay the maximum for a kid. The woman's desperate to be a mommy."

"I'll do a little more checking." Still calculating, he sank with her onto the couch.

"No harm in that, but I'm telling you, Jasper, these two are primed. No way we can lose. No way."

Mel and Sebastian became a convivial foursome with Gumm and Linda. They dined out, enjoyed the casino, lunched at the club and indulged in rousing doubles matches at tennis.

Ten days of the high life was making Mel edgy. Several times she ventured to ask Linda about the lawyer she had spoken of and was told, kindly, to be patient.

They were introduced to dozens of people. Some of them Mel found interesting and attractive, others slick and suspicious. She spent her days following the routine of a well-to-do woman with time and money on her hands.

And her nights with Sebastian.

She tried not to concern herself with her heart. She had a job to do, and if she'd fallen in love doing it, that was her problem to solve.

She knew he cared for her, just as she knew he desired her. It was a worry that he seemed so fond of the woman she pretended to be—a woman she would cease to be as soon as the job was over.

*Not quite like my Mel.* My Mel, he had said. There was hope in that, and she wasn't above clinging to it.

And as much as she wished the case were closed and justice served, she began to dread the day when they would go home, no longer married by design.

Whatever her personal needs and private hopes,

she couldn't allow herself to put them ahead of what they were trying to do.

Following a suggestion of Linda's, Mel agreed to give a party. After all, she was supposed to be an enthusiastic entertainer, a whiz of a homemaker and a society gem.

As she struggled into her little black dress, she prayed she wouldn't make some telltale faux pas that showed her up as a phony.

"Damnation," she swore as Sebastian strolled into the bedroom.

"Problem, darling?"

"Zipper's stuck." She was half in and half out of the dress, flushed, harried and mad as a cat. He was sorely tempted to help her the rest of the way out of it, rather than in.

He gave the zipper a flick that sent it up to its home, halfway up her back. "All done. You're wearing the tourmaline," he said, reaching over her shoulder to touch the stone between her breasts.

"Morgana said it was good for stress. I need all the help I can get." Turning, she slipped regretfully into the heels, which brought them eye-to-eye. "It's stupid, but I'm really nervous. The only kind of parties I've ever given involved pizza and beer. Did you see all that stuff downstairs?"

"Yes, and I also saw the caterers who will take care of it."

"But I'm, like, the hostess. I'm supposed to know what to do."

"No, you're supposed to tell other people what to do, then take all the credit."

She smiled a little. "That's not so bad. It's just that something's got to happen soon. I'll go out of my mind if it doesn't. Linda keeps making cryptic remarks about being able to help, but I feel like I've been spinning wheels for the last week."

"Patience. We take the next step tonight."

"What do you mean?" She caught at his sleeve. "We said no holding back. If you know something, have seen something, tell me."

"It doesn't always work like a perfect mirror of events. I know the person we're looking for will be here tonight, and I'll recognize who it is. We've played the game well so far, Mel. And we'll play it out."

"All right." She took a deep breath. "What do you say, honey bun? Shall we go down and get ready to greet our guests?"

He winced. "Don't call me honey bun."

"Shoot, and I thought I was getting the hang of it." She started down, then stopped with a hand pressed to her stomach. "Oh, Lord, there's the bell. Here we go."

\* \* \*

It wasn't really so bad, Mel discovered as the party flowed through the house and onto the deck. Everyone seemed to be having a dandy old time. There was some nice classical music—of Sebastian's choosing—playing in the background. The night was balmy enough that they could leave the doors wide and allow the guests to roam in and out. The food, if she did say so herself, was excellent. And, if she didn't recognize half of the canapés, it hardly mattered. She accepted the compliments graciously.

There was wine and laughter and interesting conversation. Which she supposed made for a pretty good party. And it was nice to watch Sebastian move through the room, to look over and see him smile at her, or to have him stop beside her for a touch or a private word.

Anyone looking at us would buy it, she thought. We're the world's happiest couple, madly in love with each other.

She could almost buy it herself, when his gaze moved in her direction and his eyes warmed, sending those secret signals up her spine.

Linda glided up, looking drop-dead gorgeous in a white off-the-shoulder gown. "I swear, the man can't keep his eyes off you. If I could find his twin, I might give marriage another shot after all."

"There's no one else like him," Mel said, sincerely enough. "Believe me, Donovan's one of a kind."

"And he's all yours."

"Yes. All mine."

"Well, besides being lucky in love, you throw a wonderful party. Your house is beautiful." And, Linda calculated, worth at least a good million on the market.

"Thank you, but I really owe you for recommending the caterer. He's a jewel."

"Anything I can do." She squeezed Mel's hand and gave her a long look. "I mean that."

Mel was quick. "Do you…have you… Oh, I don't mean to nag, but I haven't been able to think about anything else for days."

"No promises," she said, but then she winked. "There is someone I'd like you to meet. You did say I could invite some people."

"Of course." She slipped on her hostess mask. "You know, I feel this is your party as much as mine. You and Jasper have become such good friends."

"And we're fond of you, too. Come over this way, so I can introduce you." Keeping Mel's hand in hers, Linda began weaving through the guests. "I'll bring her back," she said, laughing. "I just need to steal her a moment. Ah, here you are, Harriet. Harriet dear, I want you to meet your hostess and my friend, Mary Ellen Ryan. Mary Ellen, Harriet Breezeport."

"How do you do?" Mel took the slim, pale hand gently. The woman was well into her sixties and had a fragile air that was accented by her snow-white hair and half glasses.

"Delighted to meet you. So kind of you to invite us." Her voice was hardly more than a whisper. "Linda told me how charming you are. This is my son, Ethan."

He was nearly as pale as his mother, and wire-thin. His handshake was brisk, and his eyes were as black as a bird's. "Lovely party."

"Thank you. Why don't I find you a chair, Mrs. Breezeport? And something to drink?"

"Oh, I would dearly love a little wine." The woman smiled wispily. "I don't want to be any bother."

"Not at all." Mel took her arm and led her to a chair. "What can I get you?"

"Oh, Ethan will take care of it. Won't you, Ethan?"

"Of course. Excuse me."

"A good boy," Harriet said as her son walked off to the buffet table. "Takes such good care of me." She smiled up at Mel. "Linda tells me you've recently moved to Tahoe."

"Yes, my husband and I moved from Seattle. It's quite a change."

"Indeed, indeed. Ethan and I sometimes vacation here. We keep a nice little condo."

They chatted while Ethan brought back a plate with a few choice canapés and a small glass of wine. Linda had already slipped off when Mel glanced over and saw Sebastian approaching.

"This is my husband." Mel slipped a hand through his arm. "Donovan, this is Harriet and Ethan Breezeport."

"Linda said you were a dashing figure." Harriet offered a hand. "I'm afraid I've been monopolizing your charming wife."

"I'm often guilty of that myself. In fact, I have to steal her for a moment. A small problem in the kitchen. Enjoy yourselves."

He nudged Mel along and then, finding no private spot, ducked with her into a closet.

"Donovan, for God's sake…"

"Shh." In the dim light, his eyes were very bright. "It's her," he said quietly.

"Who's her, and why are we standing in the closet?"

"The old woman. She's the one."

"The one?" Mel's mouth fell open. "Excuse me,

do you expect me to believe that that fragile old lady is the head of a babynapping ring?"

"Exactly." He kissed her astonished mouth. "We're closing in, Sutherland."

## Chapter 12

Mel met Harriet Breezeport twice more over the next two days, once for tea and again at a party. If it hadn't been for her faith in Sebastian, Mel would have laughed at the idea of the whispery-voiced matron as the head of a criminal organization.

But she did have faith in him, so she watched, and played her part.

It was Devereaux who fed them the information that neither Harriet nor Ethan Breezeport owned a condo in Tahoe. Nor, in fact, was there any record that either party existed.

Still, when the contact came, it came from neither of them, but from a tanned young man with a tennis racket. Mel had just finished a match with Linda and was waiting over a glass of iced tea for Sebastian to complete a round of golf with Gumm. The man approached, wearing tennis whites and a dazzling smile.

"Mrs. Ryan?"

"Yes?"

"I'm John Silbey. A mutual acquaintance pointed you out. I wonder if I could have a word with you?"

Mel hesitated, as she imagined a happily married woman might when approached by a strange man. "All right."

He sat, laying the tennis racket across his tanned knees. "I realize this is a bit unorthodox, Mrs. Ryan, but, as I said, we have mutual acquaintances. I've been told you and your husband might be interested in my services."

"Really?" She arched a brow coolly, but her heart was picking up rhythm. "You don't look like a gardener, Mr. Silbey, though my husband and I are quite desperate for one."

"No, indeed." He laughed heartily. "I'm afraid I can't help you there. I'm a lawyer, Mrs. Ryan."

"Oh?" She tried for hopeful confusion, and apparently pulled it off. Silbey leaned a little closer and spoke gently.

"This isn't the usual way I solicit clients, but when you were pointed out to me just now, I thought it might be a good opportunity for us to become acquainted. I'm told you and your husband are interested in a private adoption."

She moistened her lips and rattled the ice in her glass for good measure. "I… We've hoped," she said slowly. "We've tried. It's been very difficult. All the agencies we've tried have such long waiting lists."

"I understand."

And she could see that he did, and that he was very pleased to find her emotional, desperate and primed. He touched her hand in sympathy.

"We tried going through a lawyer before, but the whole thing fell through at the last minute." She pressed her lips together, as if to steady them. "I'm not sure I could handle that kind of disappointment again."

"It's wrenching, I'm sure. I would hate to get your hopes up before we discuss this in more detail, but I can tell you that I've represented several women who have, for one reason or another, required the placement of their children. What they want for them are good homes, loving homes. It's my job to find that,

Mrs. Ryan. And when I do, I have to say, it's one of the most rewarding experiences a man can have."

And one of the most lucrative, Mel thought, but she smiled tremulously. "We want very much to provide a good and loving home for a child, Mr. Silbey. If you could help us…I can't begin to tell you how grateful we'd be."

He touched her hand again. "Then, if you're agreeable, we'll talk further."

"We could come to your office anytime you say."

"Actually, I'd like to meet you and your husband under less restrictive circumstances. At your home, so that I can assure my client on how you live, how you are together as a couple, in your own habitat."

"Of course, of course," she said, brimming with excitement. *Don't have an office, do you, bucko?* "Whenever it's convenient for you."

"Well, I'm afraid I'm booked for the next couple of weeks."

"Oh." She didn't have to feign disappointment. "Oh, well, I suppose we've waited this long…"

He waited a moment, then smiled kindly. "I could spare an hour this evening, unless you—"

"Oh, no." She grabbed his hand in both of hers. "That would be wonderful. I'm so grateful. Donovan and I… Thank you, Mr. Silbey."

"I hope I'll be able to help. Is seven o'clock all right with you?"

"It's fine." She blinked out tears of gratitude.

When he left her, she stayed in character, certain there would be someone watching. She dabbed at her eyes with a tissue, pressed a hand to her lips. Sebastian found her sniffing into her watery iced tea.

"Mary Ellen." The sight of her red-rimmed eyes and trembling lips brought instant concern. "Darling, what's wrong?" The moment he took her hands, the jolt of excitement nearly rocked him back on his heels. Only sheer willpower kept the astonishment from showing.

"Oh, Donovan." She scrambled to her feet, spotting Gumm over his shoulder. "I'm making a scene." Laughing, she wiped at the tears. "I'm sorry, Jasper."

"Not at all." Gallantly he offered a silk handkerchief. "Has someone upset you, Mary Ellen?"

"No, no." She gave a little shuddering sob. "It's good news. Marvelous news. I'm just overreacting. Would you excuse us, Jasper? Give my regrets to Linda. I really need to speak with Donovan alone."

"Of course." He walked off to give them their privacy, and Mel buried her face in Sebastian's shoulder.

"What the hell is going on?" he demanded in a soothing murmur as he stroked her hand.

"Contact." All damp eyes and shaky smiles, she drew her head back. "This sleazy lawyer—hell, I doubt he is a lawyer—just plopped himself down and offered to help us with a private adoption. Look delighted."

"I am." He kissed her for his own enjoyment, and for the benefit of their audience. "What's the deal?"

"Out of the goodness of his heart, and in consideration of a desperate woman, he's agreed to come by tonight and discuss our needs in more detail."

"Very obliging of him."

"Oh, yes. I may not have your gifts, but I could read his mind well enough. One look at me and he thought, 'Patsy'. I could almost hear him calculating his take. Let's go home." She slipped an arm around him. "The air around here is really bad."

"Well?" Linda asked Gumm as they watched Sebastian and Mel walk away.

"Like shooting fish in a barrel." Pleased with himself, he signaled to a waiter. "They're so giddy with the idea, they'll ask the minimum amount of questions and pay the maximum fee. He might be a little more cautious, but he's so besotted with her he'd do anything to make her happy."

"Ah, love." Linda sneered. "It's the best scam in town. You got the merchandise picked out?"

Gumm ordered drinks then sat back to light a cigarette. "He wants a boy, so I think we'll oblige him, since he's paying top dollar. We've got a nurse in New Jersey ready to select a healthy male right out of the hospital."

"Good. You know, I'm fond of Mary Ellen. Maybe I'll throw her a shower."

"An excellent idea. I wouldn't be surprised if in a year or two they'd be in the market again." He checked his watch. "I'd better call Harriet and tell her she can start pushing buttons."

"Better you than me," Linda said with a grimace. "The old bag gives me the creeps."

"The old bag runs a smooth setup," he reminded her.

"Yeah, and business is business." Linda picked up the glass the waiter set in front of her and raised it in a toast. "To the happy mommy-and-daddy-to-be."

"To an easy twenty-five grand."

"Better." Linda touched her glass to his. "Much better."

Mel knew her part and was ready when Silbey arrived promptly at seven. Her hand trembled a bit as she accepted his. "I'm so glad you could come."

"It's my pleasure."

She led him into the sprawling living room, chattering brightly. "We've only been in the house a couple of weeks. There are still a lot of changes I want to make. There's a room upstairs that would make a wonderful nursery. I hope… Donovan." Sebastian stood across the room, pouring a drink. "Mr. Silbey is here."

Sebastian knew his part, as well. He appeared to be reserved and nervous as he offered Silbey a drink. After a few social inanities, they sat, Sebastian and Mel close together on the sofa, hands linked in mutual support.

All solicitude, Silbey opened his briefcase. "If I could just ask you a few questions? Get to know you a bit?"

They filled in their established backgrounds while Silbey took notes. But it was their body language that told the tale. The quick, hopeful glances exchanged, the touches. Silbey continued the interview, completely unaware that every word he spoke was being transmitted to two federal agents in an upstairs room.

Clearly pleased with the progress he was making, Silbey sent them an encouraging look. "I have to say, in my personal and professional opinion, you would make excellent parents. The selecting of a home for a child is a very delicate matter."

He pontificated for a while on stability, responsibility, and the special requirements of raising an adopted child. Mel's stomach turned even as she beamed at him.

"I can see that you've both thought this through very seriously, very thoroughly. There is, however, a point you may want to discuss at more length. The expenses. I know it sounds crass, putting a price on something we should consider a miracle. But there is a reality to be accepted. There's a matter of medical expenses and compensation to the mother, my fee, court costs and filing—all of which I will handle."

"We understand," Sebastian said, wishing he was free to wring Silbey's neck.

"I'll require a twenty-five-thousand-dollar retainer, and another hundred and twenty-five thousand at the end of the legalities. This will include all the expenses of the mother."

Sebastian started to speak. He was, after all, a businessman. But Mel gripped his hand tighter and hit him with a pleading glance.

"The money won't be a problem," he said, and touched her cheek.

"All right then." Silbey smiled. "I have a client. She's very young, unmarried. She wants very much to finish college, and has come to the difficult decision that raising a child on her own would make this impossible. I'll be able to provide you with her medical background, and that of the father. She's quite firm that there be no other information divulged. With your permission, I will tell her about you, and give her my recommendation."

"Oh." Mel pressed her fingers to her lips. "Oh, yes."

"To be frank, you're exactly the kind of parents she was hoping for. I believe we'll be able to complete this with everyone's best interest served."

"Mr. Silbey." Mel leaned her head against Sebastian's shoulder. "When…I mean, how soon would we know? And the child— What can you tell us?"

"I'd say you'd know within forty-eight hours. As far as the child…" He smiled benignly. "My client is due to deliver any day. I have a feeling my call is going to ease her mind tremendously."

By the time they had walked Silbey to the door, Mel had shed a few more tears. The moment she was alone with Sebastian, fury burned her eyes dry.

"That sonofa—"

"I know." He put his hands on her shoulders. She was vibrating like a plucked string. "We'll get them, Mel. We'll get them all."

"You're damn right we will." She paced to the stairs and back. "You know what this means, don't you? They're going to steal a baby, an infant, probably right out of a hospital or clinic."

"Logical as always," he murmured, watching her carefully.

"I can't stand it." She pressed a hand to her churning stomach. "I can't bear the idea of some poor woman lying in a hospital bed being told her baby's been stolen."

"It won't take long." He wanted to slip into her thoughts, to see for himself just what was in her head. But he'd given his word. "We have to play this through."

"Yeah." That was just what she was going to do. He wouldn't approve, she decided. And neither would the feds. But there were times you had to follow your heart. "We'd better make sure the boys upstairs got all of that." She took a deep breath. "Then I think we should do what any happy, expectant couple would do."

"Which is?"

"Go out and tell our dearest friends. And celebrate."

Mel sat in the lounge at the Silver Palace with a glass of champagne in her hand and a smile on her lips. "To new and valued friends."

Linda laughed and clinked glasses. "Oh, no, to the happy parents-to-be."

"We'll never be able to thank you." She looked from Linda to Gumm. "Both of you."

"Nonsense." Gumm patted her hand. "Linda merely made an inquiry to a friend. We're both delighted such a small gesture reaped such benefits."

"We still have to sign papers," Sebastian pointed out. "And wait for the mother's approval."

"We're not going to worry about any of that." Linda waved details away. "What we have to do now is plan a baby shower. I'd love to give you one, Mary Ellen, up in the penthouse."

Though she was getting damned tired of weeping, Mel let her eyes fill. "That's so…" Tears spilled over as she got to her feet. "Excuse me." An emotional wreck, she rushed off to the ladies' room. As she'd hoped, Linda followed her a moment later.

"What an idiot I am."

"Don't be silly." Linda sat beside her, slipped an arm around her. "They say expectant mothers are apt to cry at the drop of a hat."

With a shaky laugh, Mel dried her eyes. "I suppose. Would you mind terribly getting me a drink of water before I try to repair the damage?"

"Sit right there."

Mel figured she had twenty seconds at best, so she moved fast. She flipped open Linda's beaded evening bag, pushed through past lipstick and perfume and gripped the penthouse key. She was slipping it into

the pocket of her evening pants when Linda came
back with a cup.

"Thanks." Mel smiled up at her. "Thanks a lot."

The next step was to get away from the group for
at least twenty minutes without being detected. She
suggested a celebratory dinner, with a little gambling
as an appetizer. Always the gracious host, Gumm
insisted on making the arrangements in the dining
room himself. Marking time, Mel managed to slip
away from Sebastian and Linda in the crowd at the
crap table.

She took the express elevator, keeping well to the
back of the glass walls. The top floor was silent as
she stepped out. Mel checked her watch, then fit the
key into the lock of the penthouse.

She didn't need much. With the evidence they
already had, she needed only enough to link Gumm
and Linda with Silbey or the Breezeports. She judged
Gumm as a man who kept records on everything—
and kept them cleverly.

Maybe it was rash, she thought as she headed
straight for a huge ebony desk. But the idea of them
even now plotting to steal a baby fired her blood. She
wasn't going to stand by while someone else went
through what Rose and Stan had experienced. Not

while there was a chance she could make a difference.

She found nothing in the desk of interest and used up five of her allotted twenty minutes in the search. Undaunted, she moved on, checking tables for false bottoms, locating a wall safe behind a section of books. She would have loved to have the time and the talent to lift that lock, but she had to admit defeat. With less than three minutes to go, she found what she was looking for in plain sight.

The second bedroom of the suite served as a fussily decorated office that Linda used as a convenience. There, on top of her French provincial desk, was a leather-bound account book.

At first glance, it seemed like nothing more than it purported to be, a daily record of deliveries for the hotel shops. Mel had nearly put it down again in disgust when she noted the dates.

Merchandise acquired 1/21. Tampa. Picked up 1/22. Little Rock. Delivered 1/23. Louisville. Accepted COD 1/25. Detroit. Commission 10,000.

Breathing shallowly, Mel flipped pages.

Merchandise acquired 5/5. Monterey. Picked up 5/6. Scuttlefield. 5/7. Delivered 5/8. Lubbock. Accepted COD 5/11. Atlanta. Commission 12,000.

David, she thought, and didn't bother to hold back

a string of oaths. It was right there, all the dates and cities. And more. Babies listed like packages to be shipped and paid for on delivery.

Tight-lipped, she skimmed the pages and let out a hiss between her teeth.

H.B. ordered new blue package, Bloomfield, New Jersey. Pick up between 8/22 and 8/25. Standard route, acceptance and final payment expected by 8/31. Estimated commission 25,000.

"You bitch," Mel muttered as she closed the book. She struggled against the urge to break something, and scanned the room instead. When she was certain nothing was out of place, she started for the door.

"Oh, she's probably off having another crying jag," Linda said as she walked through the main door of the penthouse into the parlor. "He'll find her."

Mel took a quick look around and opted for the closet.

"I can't say I'm looking forward to spending the evening with her," Gumm said. "I doubt she'll talk about anything but booties and baby formula."

"We can take it, lover. Especially for twice our usual fee." Her voice faded a bit as she walked toward the opposite bedroom. "I think it was a good idea to arrange for dinner up here. The more grateful and emotional they are, the less they'll think. Once they have the kid, they won't question anything."

"Harriet's thoughts exactly. She already has Ethan putting the wheels in motion. I was surprised when she came down to take a look at them for herself, but she's a little more cautious since the Frost affair."

Mel kept her breath slow and even. She pressed her fingers against the stone of her ring. Communication between people who are important to each other, she remembered, and shut her eyes. Well, here's hoping. Come on, Donovan, get your butt up here and bring the marines.

It was risky, she knew, but she thought the odds were in her favor. Reaching into her bag, she felt the comforting bulk of her weapon. Not that way. She took a deep, bracing breath and put the account book in instead of taking the revolver out. She set her bag on the floor, then opened the closet.

"They'll pass the merchandise to our contact in Chicago," Gumm was saying.

"I'd like to pick him up in Albuquerque," Linda put in. "I could always use an extra couple of thousand for the run." Her head snapped up as Mel deliberately bumped a chair. "What the hell?"

Gumm was in the room like a shot, twisting the

struggling Mel's arms behind her. "Let me go! Jasper, you're hurting me."

"People who break into other people's homes often get hurt."

"I—I was just lying down for a while." She made her eyes dart crazily to make the lie all the more ridiculous. "I didn't think you'd mind."

"What have we got here?" Linda asked.

"A plant. I should have known. I should have smelled it."

"Cop?" Linda considered.

"Cop?" Eyes wide with alarm, Mel twisted. "I don't know what you're talking about. I was just resting."

"How'd she get in?" Jasper demanded, and Mel let the key she was holding slip out of her hands.

"Mine." Swearing in disgust, Linda bent to pick it up. "She must have palmed it."

"I don't know what—" Jasper cut off Mel's protest with a backhand that left her head ringing. She decided it was time to drop one act for another.

"Okay, okay, you don't have to play rough." She shuddered and swallowed audibly. "I'm just doing my job."

Jasper shoved her into the parlor and onto the sofa. "Which is?"

"Look, I'm just an actress. I took a gig with

Donovan. He's a PI." Stall, Mel thought. Stall, stall, stall, because he was coming. She knew he was. "I only did what he told me to do. I don't care what you're into. And I've got an appreciation for a good scam."

Gumm moved to the desk and took a pistol from the top drawer. "What are you doing in here?"

"Man, you don't need that," she said, swallowing. "He said I should get the key and come up to look around. He thought there might be some papers in the desk there." She gestured toward the ebony desk. "It seemed like a real kick, you know. And he's paying me five grand for the job."

"A two-bit actress and a PI," Linda said furiously. "What the hell do we do now?"

"What we have to do."

"Look, look, you say the word and I'm out of here. I mean out of the state." Mel tried for a tawdry kind of charm. "I mean, it was great while it lasted, the clothes and all, but I don't want any trouble. I didn't hear anything, I didn't see anything."

"You heard plenty," Gumm countered.

"I got a bad memory."

"Shut up," Linda snapped, and Mel shrugged.

"We'll have to contact Harriet. She's back in Baltimore seeing to the details of the last job." Gumm ran his hands through his hair. "She's going to be very unhappy. She'll have to call off the nurse. We can't take a kid without a buyer."

"Twenty-five thousand down the tubes." Linda sent Mel a look of avid dislike. "I was actually pretty fond of you, Mary Ellen." She walked over to lean into Mel's face, squeezing a hand around her throat. "As it is now, I'm going to get a lot of satisfaction out of letting Jasper take care of you."

"Hey, listen..."

"Shut up." She shoved Mel back. "You'd better arrange for someone to do it tonight. And to pick up the PI, too. I think a little spat in their house, maybe. A nice murder-suicide."

"I'll take care of it."

At the knock on the door, Mel made to scramble up and as expected had Linda clamp a hand over her mouth.

"Room service, Mr. Gumm."

"The damn dinner," he muttered. "Take her into the other room and keep her quiet. I'll handle this."

"A pleasure." Linda took the gun Gumm handed her and gestured Mel into the next room.

Smoothing back his hair, Gumm went to the door, then gestured for the waiter to roll in the room-service tray. "Don't bother to set up. Our guests haven't arrived yet."

"Yes, they have." Sebastian strolled in. "Jasper, I'd like you to meet Special Agent Devereaux. FBI."

In the next room, Linda swore and Mel grinned. "Excuse me," she said politely, tramped hard on Linda's foot and knocked the gun aside.

"Sutherland," Sebastian said with restrained fury from the doorway. "You've got some explaining to do."

"In a minute." To please herself, she turned and rammed her fist into Linda's astonished face. "That one was for Rose," she said.

He wasn't happy with her. Sebastian made that abundantly clear through the rest of that evening, through all the explanations. Devereaux wasn't exactly thrilled himself, though she thought it was small-minded of him, since she'd all but wrapped the evidence in a bow and handed it to him.

Sebastian had a right to be annoyed, she supposed. She'd acted on her own. But she was the professional. Besides, it had worked out exactly as she'd planned, so what was his problem?

She asked him just that several times, as they packed up for the trip home, as they flew back to Monterey, as he dropped her off at her office.

His only answer was one of his long, enigmatic

looks. The last thing he said to her left her miserable and silent.

"I kept my word, Mary Ellen. You didn't. As a matter of trust, it comes down to that."

That had been two days before, she thought as she brooded at her desk. And there hadn't been a peep from him since.

She'd even swallowed her pride and called him, only to get his answering machine. It wasn't that she felt she owed him an apology, exactly. But she did think he deserved another chance to be reasonable.

She toyed with the idea of going to Morgana or Anastasia and asking them to intercede. But that was too weak. All she wanted to do was to put things back on an even keel between them.

No, no, she wanted much more than that, Mel admitted. And that was what was killing her.

Only one way to do it, she told herself, and kicked back from her desk. She would hunt him down, pin him to the wall if necessary, but she would make him listen to her.

All the way along the winding mountain road she practiced what she would say and how she would say it. She tried being tough, experimented with being quiet and solemn, and even took a shot at being penitent. When that didn't sit well, she opted for aggressive tactics. She'd just march right up to his door and tell him to cut out the silent routine. She was tired of it.

If he wasn't there, she'd wait.

He was there, all right, she discovered as she reached the top of his lane. But he certainly wasn't alone. There were three other cars in the drive, including what appeared to be the longest stretch limo in the known world.

She stepped out of her car and stood beside it, wondering what to do next.

"I told you, didn't I tell you?" Mel looked around and spotted a pretty woman in a flowing tea-length dress. "A green-eyed blonde," she said, a definite smack of satisfaction in her Irish voice. "I told you something was bothering him."

"Yes, dear." The man beside her was tall and gangly, his graying hair receding into a dramatic widow's peak. He looked rather dashing in jodhpurs and top boots. A Victorian quizzing glass dangled from a string around his neck. "But it was I who told you it was a female."

"Nevertheless." The woman glided across the grounds with both plump hands held out to Mel. "Hello, hello, and welcome."

"Ah, thanks. I'm, ah, looking for…"

"Of course you are," the woman said with a breezy laugh. "Anyone could see that, couldn't they, Douglas?"

"Pretty," he said in response. "Not a pushover." He peered at her with eyes that were so much like Sebastian's that Mel began to put two and two together. "He didn't tell us about you, which speaks for itself."

"I suppose," she said after a moment. His parents, she thought, sinking. A family reunion was no place for a confrontation. "I don't want to disturb him when he has company. Maybe you could tell him I stopped by."

"Nonsense. I'm Camilla, by the way. Sebastian's mother." She took Mel's arm and began to lead her toward the house. "I quite understand your being in love with him, my dear child. I've loved him myself for years."

Panicked, Mel looked for a route of escape. "No, I— That is…I really think I should come back later."

"No time like the present," Douglas said, and gave her a friendly nudge through the door. "Sebastian, look what we've brought you." He brought the glass to his eye and peered around owlishly. "Where is that boy?"

"Upstairs." Morgana breezed in from the direction of the kitchen. "He'll be… Oh, hello."

"Hi." The frost on the greeting told Mel it had been a bad idea to come. "I was just…leaving. I didn't realize your family was visiting."

"Oh, they drop in now and again." After she took one long look into Mel's eyes, Morgana's smile warmed. "Stepped in it, did you?" she murmured. "That's all right. He'll come around."

"I really think I should—"

"Meet the rest of the family," Camilla said gaily and kept Mel's arm in an iron grip as she marched her toward the kitchen.

There were glorious scents in the air, and roomsful of people. A tall, queenly woman was laughing raucously as she stirred something on the stove. Nash was on a stool beside a lean middle-aged man with steel-gray hair. When the man glanced up at her, she felt like a moth on a pin.

"Hey, Mel." Nash sent her a wave, and she was thrust into the fray. Introductions followed, Camilla taking charge territorially.

"My brother-in-law, Matthew," she began, gesturing to the man beside Nash. "My sister Maureen at the stove." Maureen waved an absent hand and sniffed at her brew. "And my sister, Bryna."

"Hello." A woman every bit as stunning as Morgana stepped forward to take Mel's hand. "I hope you're not too befuddled by all this. We all dropped in quite unexpectedly just this morning."

"No, no, really. I don't want to intrude. I should really just—"

Then it was too late. Sebastian walked in, flanked by Ana and a short, husky man with twinkling eyes.

"Ah, Sebastian." Bryna kept Mel's hand. "More company. Mel, this is Padrick, Ana's father."

"Hello." It was easier to look at him than Sebastian. "Nice to meet you."

He strolled right up and pinched her cheek. "Stay for dinner. We'll put some meat on your bones. Maureen, my moonflower, what is that tantalizing scent?"

"Hungarian goulash."

Padrick winked at Mel. "And not a single eye of newt in the batch. Guaranteed."

"Yes, well, I appreciate the invitation, but I really can't stay." She took a chance and glanced at Sebastian. "I'm sorry," she fumbled when he just continued to gaze at her with those quiet, inscrutable eyes. "I shouldn't have… I mean, I really should have called first. I'll catch you later."

"Excuse us," he said to the group at large, gripping Mel's arm as she tried to dash by. "Mel hasn't seen the foal since the birthing."

Though she knew it was cowardly, she shot one

desperate glance behind her as he pulled her out of the door. "You have company."

And that company moved as a unit to the kitchen window to watch the goings-on.

"Family isn't company," he said. "And, since you've come all this way, I have to believe you have something to say."

"Well, I do, and I'll say it when you stop dragging me."

"Fine." He stopped near the paddock where the foal was busily nursing. "Say it."

"I wanted to… I talked to Devereaux. He said Linda copped a plea and spilled everything. They've got enough on Gumm and the Breezeports to put them away for a long time. They've got a line on a handful of others, like Silbey, too."

"I'm aware of all that."

"Oh, well, I wasn't sure." She stuck her hands in her pockets. "It's going to take some time to locate all the children, and get them back where they belong, but… It worked, damn it," she blurted out. "I don't know what the hell you're so bent out of shape about."

His voice was deceptively mild. "Don't you?"

"I did what I thought was best." She kicked at the ground, then strode over to the fence. "They'd already made plans to snatch another kid. It was right in the book."

"The book you went in and found. On your own."

"If I'd told you what I was going to do, you'd have tried to stop me."

"Wrong. I would have stopped you."

She frowned back at him. "See? By doing it my way, we saved a lot of heartache."

"And risked more." The anger he'd been struggling to hold back flared. "There was a bruise on your cheek."

"A qualified job risk," she shot back. "And it's my cheek."

"Good God, Sutherland. She had a gun on you."

"Only for a minute. Hell, Donovan, the day I can't handle a sap like Linda Glass is the day I retire. I'm telling you I just couldn't take the idea of them snatching another baby, so I went with the gut." Her eyes were so eloquent, some of his anger died. "I know what I'm doing, and I also know it seems like I was cutting you out. But I wasn't. I called you."

He took a calming breath, but it failed to work. "And if I'd been too late?"

"Well, you weren't, so what's the point?"

"The point is, you didn't trust me."

"The hell I didn't. Who else was I trusting when I

stood in that closet and tried to use the ring or whatever connection we had to get you and the feds up there? If I hadn't trusted you, I would've slipped right out the door with the book." She grabbed at his shirt and shook him. "It was because I trusted you that I played it out that way. Staying there, letting them catch me—because I knew I could trust you to back me up. I tried to explain it all to you before. I knew they'd tell me things Devereaux could use, and with the book as a backup, we'd have them cold."

Steadying himself, he turned away. As angry as he was, he saw the truth in that. Perhaps it wasn't the kind of trust he'd wanted, but it was trust. "You could have been hurt."

"Sure. I could be hurt every time I take a case. That's what I do. That's what I am." She swallowed, struggling to clear an obstruction in her throat. "I had to accept you, and what you are. And believe me, it was no snap. If we're going to be…friends, the same goes."

"You may have a point. But I still don't like your style."

"Fine," she snapped back, blinking her vision clear. "Same goes."

At the kitchen window, Camilla shook her head. "He always was stubborn."

"Ten pounds she wears him down." Padrick pinched his wife's bottom affectionately. "Ten pounds and no tricks."

Ana shushed him. "We won't be able to hear."

Mel let out a shaky breath. "Well, we know where we stand anyway. And I'm sorry."

"Excuse me?" He turned and was astonished by the tears he saw on her face. "Mary Ellen—"

"Don't. I'm going to get this out." She wiped furiously at the tears. "I have to do what I think is right. And I still think what I did was right, but I'm sorry you're so angry with me, because I... Oh, I hate this." She scrubbed her hands over her face, evading him when he reached for her. "Don't. I don't want you to. I don't need to be patted or soothed, even if I am acting like a baby. You were mad, and I guess I can't blame you for it, or for dropping me cold."

"Dropping you cold?" He nearly laughed. "I left you alone, and well out of harm's way, until I could be certain I could restrain myself from throttling you or present you with an ultimatum you might have tossed back in my face."

"Whatever." She sniffed and regained some control. "I guess what I did hurt you, and I didn't mean it to."

He smiled a little. "Same goes."

"Okay." There had to be some way to finish this with a little dignity intact. "Anyway, I wanted to clear the air, and to tell you I think we did a good job. Now that it's done, I figured I'd better return this." It was hard, one of the hardest things she'd ever done, to pull his ring from her finger. "Looks like the Ryans are getting a divorce."

"Yes." He took the ring back and held it warm in the palm of his hand as he considered her. It wasn't necessary to dip into her thoughts to see that she was suffering. It wasn't particularly noble, but the fact that she was pleased him very much. "It seems a pity." He brushed his knuckles over her cheek. "Then again, I much prefer you to her."

She blinked. "You do?"

"Very much. I was beginning to find her a little dull. She'd never argue with me, and she was forever having her nails done." Gently he cupped a hand behind her head and drew her closer. "She certainly wouldn't have been caught dead in those jeans."

"Guess not," she murmured, leaning into him, into the kiss.

She felt herself tremble, felt the tears welling up again as she threw her arms around him. "Sebastian. I need…" She tightened her hold as her lips clung to his.

"Tell me."

"I want— Oh, Lord, you scare me." She drew back, her eyes wet and terrified. "Just read my mind, will you? For God's sake, just look at what I'm feeling and give me a break."

His eyes darkened, his hands moved up to cup her face. He looked, and found everything he'd been waiting for. "Again," he murmured, taking her mouth. But this time the kiss was gentle, coaxing. "Can't you tell me? Can't you say the words? They're the truest magic."

"I don't want you to feel like I'm boxing you in. It's just that I…"

"I love you," he finished for her.

"Yeah." She managed a weak smile. "You could say I blurred the lines. I wasn't going to bring it up, but it seemed like I should. Only fair that I should be up-front. Pretty awkward when you've got a houseful of people."

"All of whom have their noses pressed up to the kitchen window and are enjoying this nearly as much as I."

"Who—?" She spun around, flushed and stumbled backward. "Oh, Lord. Look, I'm going. I really can't believe I did this." Unnerved, she lifted a hand to tug at her hair. And saw the ring back on her finger. As she stared at it, he stepped forward.

"I gave the stone to Morgana. A stone I've treasured most of my life. I asked her to have a ring made out of it. For you. For you," he repeated, waiting until she lifted her eyes to his. "Because you were the only woman I wanted to wear it. You were the only woman I wanted to share my life with. Twice now I've put it on your finger, and both times it was a pledge to you." He held out his hand, offering. "No one, in any time, in any place, will love you more."

Her eyes were dry now, and her nerves were suddenly calm as the day. "Do you mean it?"

His lips curved. "No, Sutherland. I'm lying."

With a laugh, she launched herself into his arms. "Tough break. I've got witnesses." The spontaneous applause from the kitchen made her laugh again. "Oh, I do love you, Donovan. I'm going to do my best to make your life eventful."

He swung her in one giddy circle. "I know." After one last long kiss, he took her by the hand. "Come, meet your family again. We've all been waiting for you."

\* \* \* \* \*

*Don't miss the next magical instalment in*
**The Donovan Legacy**

Charmed
*by*
Nora Roberts

*Anastasia Donovan knew that her gift marked
her as different, special – perhaps even dangerous.
She had spent years hiding herself from the world,
terrified about the consequences of revealing
what she really was.*

*When Boone Sawyer came into her life, bent on
finding out the truth about her, Anastasia had
to protect herself and her magic at all costs. She
would keep her secrets whatever it took.*

*Then she was confronted with a terrifying threat to
everything she had learned to love. With a child's
future at stake, Anastasia could not deny her
powers, even if it meant risking her own life.*

*Read on for a preview!*

# CHARMED

Magic exists. Who can doubt it, when there are rainbows and wildflowers, the music of the wind and the silence of the stars? Anyone who has loved has been touched by magic. It is such a simple and such an extraordinary part of the lives we live.

There are those who have been given more, who have been chosen to carry on a legacy handed down through endless ages. Their forebears were Merlin the enchanter, Ninian the sorceress, the faerie princess Rhiannon, the Wegewarte of Germany and the jinns of Arabia. Through their blood ran the power of Finn of the Celts, the ambitious Morgan le Fay, and others whose names were whispered only in shadows and in secret.

When the world was young and magic as common as a raindrop, faeries danced in the deep forests, and – sometimes for mischief, sometimes for love – mixed with mortals.

And they do still.

Her bloodline was old. Her power was ancient. Even as a child she had understood, had been taught, that such gifts were not without price. The loving parents who treasured her could not lower the cost, or pay it themselves, but could only love, instruct and watch the young girl grow to womanhood. They could only stand and hope as she experienced the pains and the joys of that most fascinating of journeys.

And, because she felt more than others, because her gift demanded that she feel more, she learned to court peace.

As a woman, she preferred a quiet life, and was often alone without the pain of loneliness.

As a witch, she accepted her gift, and never forgot the responsibility it entailed.

Perhaps she yearned, as mortals and others have yearned since the beginning, for a true and abiding love. For she knew better than most that there was no power, no enchantment, no sorcery, greater than the gift of an open and accepting heart.

**Passion. Power. Suspense.**
**It's time to fall under the spell of Nora Roberts.**